3-8-88
15.95
Baker & Taylor

FOOL'S SANCTUARY

FOOL'S
SANCTUARY

by

Jennifer Johnston

VIKING

VIKING
Viking Penguin Inc.
40 West 23rd Street,
New York, New York 10010, U.S.A.

First American Edition
Published in 1988

LIBRARY OF CONGRESS CATALOGING IN PUBLICATION DATA
Johnston, Jennifer, 1930–
Fool's sanctuary.
I. Title.
PR6060.0394F6   1988   823′.914   87-40234
ISBN 0-670-81783-X

Printed in the United States of America by
Arcata Graphics, Fairfield, Pennsylvania
Set in Times Roman

For S.R.
with laughter and rage
and love remembered

FOOL'S SANCTUARY

There are no new days ahead of me.

Is this what they meant by limbo?

Waiting time, floating time, time for snatching at the comfortable and uncomfortable moments of the past.

Why do I die is not the question. All fools know the answer to that one.

But how?

How has my life led me to this moment?

There is no day, no night, here.

The river is wide and slow.

They pluck from time to time at the remains of my body with their kind, warm hands.

Their voices flow, a counter-stream across me.

As yet, I hear no voice from God.

I do pray from time to time that when, or should I say if, there is some revelation of heaven, it won't be like living eternally through *Songs of Praise*.

I don't want to meet all my loved ones again, their faces burnished with soulfulness and goodwill; if I have to come across them, I want them to be as they were, undiminished by the eternal joys of heaven.

I can still laugh at myself.

Deo gratias.

Paradise holds out no charms for me.

I said to Cathal once . . . yes, to Cathal . . . only to him would I have said such a romantic thing, that I would be a ghost here, along with all the others. He laughed. I remember the sound of his laugh. I remember the evening sun hurling its light across the water. The memory hurts my eyes.

The ghosts here have always been so solitary, no carousals or laughter; distant doors close, steps move past you on the stairs, someone will sigh. Well-ordered, you might call them, but not unhappy. Perhaps they are all content to pass eternity here at Termon, their sanctuary.

I have wondered from time to time over the last few years, what will become of this house; this white elephant.

Thirty years ago it would have been bought by the nuns, but they're selling the convents now.

A country house hotel maybe? I suppose it could have a worse fate.

If anyone were to ask me I would say that I would rather it were just left to fall down. Isn't that terrible of me? How everyone would disapprove. Feckless, thoughtless, typical of Miranda, they would say.

A romantic ruin full of ghosts. The children and young people from the village and roundabout would make daring trips, hoping against hope to see or hear something that would set their hearts racing with fear and excitement. Stories upon stories would be told, truths and half-truths argued over. That would be the most acceptable solution for the ghosts. Then the house would truly become their sanctuary.

I am not nostalgic for old times.

Things are different now, better perhaps in some ways. Yes, yes of course better.

People have freedom. That was what everyone wanted.

I think it was. That was the word they used.

I used it too.

I talked wildly about freedom.

I felt briefly at one time a longing to fight for freedom, but I merely cried for freedom; an inadequate contribution to the struggles of a nation.

I am laughing.

Can't you hear me laughing?

Their hands adjust the covers, smooth my hair.

They cannot hear me laughing.

They would be upset if they could hear me.

They would be sure to consider it a manifestation of physical pain and they would in their kindness inject me with drugs. A stinging in the wrist or my backside and I would be relieved. My head, even, is lost to me when they do that in their kindness. I can no longer see or hear the images of the past. Then, I am lonely, afraid. So I try not to upset them in any way.

I can call them all to my side now, as I was never able to through my living years.

Father.

Andrew.

Nanny.

Harry.

Cathal.

The cast of my play. The play that is in my head, always in my head.

Mother?

Mother, whose lingering presence was so strong for the others, was, and still is for me, merely a series of sharply recollected sounds in my head; the swish of a dress in my nursery bedroom as she crossed the floor to kiss me goodnight, the tapping of her shoes on the flagstones of the hall; the sound of the piano playing, always playing, summer and winter, afternoon and evening, music always, always drifting through the air.

Au clair de la lune,
Mon ami Pierrot,
Prête-moi ta plume
Pour écrire un mot.
Ma chandelle est morte;
Je n'ai plus de feu.
Ouvre-moi ta porte,
Pour l'amour de Dieu.

I didn't know what the words meant, but I sang them obediently for her each evening, before climbing the stairs with Nanny to my room.

Nanny didn't know what the words meant either.

'Don't always be asking questions. It's a song that's what it is.'

She herself would sing me songs, in Irish as well as English.

Songs that grew inside my bones and head; incomprehensible, sorrowful words.

ImBeal Atha na Gár atá an stáid bhrea mhóduil . . . . No, this is not the time for Nanny's song.

'Don't always be asking questions. You're a holy terror for asking questions.'

No.

Mother is not among my cast.

Of course, if Mother had been alive, had been with us that weekend nothing would have been the same. I would not have been the same Miranda, nor Cathal the same Cathal. Idiotic really to muse on such things. We are faced all the time with the indelible reality of the past. Even if we dare to shut our eyes to the truth, it is still there waiting to outface us when we open them again; if we open them again, perhaps I should have said.

Maybe I should have married after all; raised a great brood of children, if only to keep this place alive and kicking, save it from the gombeen men; or the nuns, or the country house hotel crowd.

But I didn't allow myself that freedom.

There were times when I cursed myself and God and even Nanny for the position in which I had landed myself, times of real loneliness and pain; so often I longed to do a bunk, like Andrew, get away, like any sane person might have done.

Yes, get away.

But here I am still and it's all over now.

When Father died in 1939 the little church was full.

Luckily it was a warm spring day and our Catholic friends and neighbours and tenants stood outside in the sun waiting for the service to end. The church smelt of the dust that had heated and cooled with the years on the central heating pipes, of Brasso and of all the funeral flowers heaped along the altar steps. Andrew and I stood in the front pew, he sleek and upright, his face like the face of a ghost.

> The day Thou gavest Lord is ended,
> The darkness falls at Thy behest;
> To Thee our morning hymns ascended,
> Thy praise shall hallow now our rest.

So lonely, he looked, so pale. Pale ghost, I see you now.

> The sun that bids us rest is waking
> Our brethren neath the western sky,
> And hour by hour fresh lips are making
> Thy wondrous doings heard on high.

'Sing loud,' I said. 'Please Andrew, sing loud.'

He opened his mouth and for the first time in our lives did something that I had asked him to do.

> So be it Lord, Thy throne shall never
> Like earth's proud empires, pass away.

I could hear the people outside the church singing also.

I remember hoping briefly that they wouldn't be excommunicated.

5

But stand and rule and grow forever,
Till all Thy creatures own Thy sway.

When he kissed me goodbye his lips were cold and his eyes burned like the windows of the house in the evening sun.

'Are you all right?' I asked.

He held me tight against him for a moment.

'I don't want to come back. Ever, Miranda. Don't make things hard for me.'

I laughed.

So unkind.

We laugh in this country for such strange reasons.

I didn't understand his pain until it was too late.

I suppose I was the only one who might have persuaded him to come back, but I didn't realise that until it was too late either.

It takes so long to learn.

It's the fumbling I have hated; painful groping through grey light, the only certainty being that you will arrive at this gate.

In a hundred years from now no one here will remember my name, nor Father's.

His trees will have been cut down by then. His reclaimed land will still be farmed, rich fertile land, but no one will remember that once it was sand and bent grass, beautiful desolation. Maybe even the little church will have become a super market or a craft shop; that sort of transformation is happening all over the place these days. Perhaps some lovers of the curious will have collected father's pamphlets on re-afforestation and land reclamation; his meticulous maps of these townlands, his notes like black ants crawling on the margins. Perhaps they will become collector's items. He would have been amused by such a thought.

Henry Augustus Martin, collector's item.

I won't even leave that mark.

I walked like King Wenceslas's page, in his footsteps leaving no trace of my own.

It was so easy to do that.

6

I lost my taste for danger when they killed Cathal. After that I chose my road. At the time it seemed the right thing to do, creep in Father's warmth; avoid confrontation with the world. Of course, looking back from here, I see how wrong I was.

I should have battered at their doors.

Gutless.

As gutless as the men who took Cathal away that night and shot him in the head.

I looked for heroes then.

Those men were the heroes that I got.

Better keep quiet.

Better not think such thoughts.

Better not waste what little energy I have on bitterness.

They move again. I hear their whispers and the soft rustling of their clothes.

They are ready. The tears are waiting behind their eyes. I will be washed from their lives. Soon. Kind lives. Kind hands. Kind murmuring voices.

I am almost ready.

Just one more time I must assemble the cast. I must search for the clue. Maybe there is no clue. Maybe the truth is anarchy. Maybe there is no truth. Maybe there is only pain.

No.

They move away now. They are the ghosts now. Their arms rise and fall. Their voices rustle. They fade into the darkness beyond my knowing.

I am alone.

It is time to begin.

Father

Andrew

Nanny

Harry

and Cathal.

Still, golden afternoon.

The sun leaning towards evening, casting long evening shadows. The leaves already changing colour. No more green among the branches.

That which gives an Indian Summer its memorable quality is the warmth of the colours as well as the unexpected warmth of the air.

The cycle is for a short while disrupted; even time seems to pause.

Seems to pause.

The clocks cease to tick.

We live for a few days, a week even, through an unearned respite.

Through the stillness sliced the whistle of the train; its energy startling the peace.

This perfection is an accident, an aberration. Termon belongs to the world. The cycle will re-commence, has, in fact already begun to do so.

Miranda heard the whistle and put the top on her fountain pen.

Though the office was on the wrong side of the house to get the evening sun it was still warm, stuffy, full of dust. The maids were never allowed in here to clean, so, thought Miranda, even the dust was antique. From time to time Mr Dillon took a broom to the place and swept the mouse droppings and decayed spiders' webs out into the yard, stirring the lazy dust as he did so which then settled again on the books and papers and on the big mahogany desk.

I hate figures, she thought, as she screwed the top of the ink bottle. I hate adding and totting and multiplying. It gives me a headache and inky fingers. I hate writing boring figures down into these account books, lines and lines of boring figures and boring words, and boring, boring facts.

I wonder will Cathal like my hair, or be angry. Father hasn't noticed. He hasn't said he's noticed. That probably means he doesn't like it. Cathal will notice.

She rubbed at the ink on one of her fingers.

8

If he comes.

He'll come. He has to come.

My head feels light, not just from losing a weight of hair, but from the weight of figures. A paradox.

Is that what you'd call a paradox?

I am such an ignoramus.

'Miranda.'

It was Nanny calling.

Amazing how her old voice had so much carrying power.

She has heard the train too. Old hawk ears. That's why she's calling me; to let me know she knows my innermost thoughts.

Old hawk brain.

She'll shake her finger in my eye, that's what she'll do.

'Miranda.'

The yard was warm and smelling sweetly of horses.

Not a breath of wind stirred her shingled hair or the golden leaves on the chestnut trees outside the gate.

'Miranda.'

She never has to be told anything. She knows everything that goes on in the whole world. She knows bad thoughts, good thoughts, nothing escapes her hawk eyes.

'Coming.'

She ran across the lawn below the house.

'Coming, coming, coming.'

The old woman was sitting on her usual summer seat under an oak tree by the path that ran down to the beach. When the sun was shining it was warmer there than in the house, she always said, and now she had need of all the warmth she could get. From her seat she could keep her hawk eyes on the movements of the maids opening and closing the windows to let warm fresh air into the house, the boy weeding the long border on one side of the lawn and the kitchen yard, where in her opinion the cook wasted too much time talking to the gardener when he brought the vegetables up to the door . . . and of course the comings and goings of Miranda. Her knitting bag was beside her on the seat, her fingers twitched fretfully in her lap. Her fingers had once been deft, but had become in the last few years arthritic, painful and clumsy. She no longer had control over the needles and fine soft wool. To her anger and slight shame, she now had to fumble with the largest needles and thick strands of wool.

'Blankets and shawls are all I'm fit for now,' she would mutter, as if reproaching herself for her own inabilities.

'I called you,' she said, as Miranda appeared beside her. 'I called and called.'

'I heard you. I answered you. I came.'

'I like people to jump when I call them.'

'I jumped. Don't I always jump? You have me very well trained.'

'Ttttt.'

'What did you call me for, anyway?'

'I'm out of wool. I need another skein wound. Sit down there now and hold it for me.'

'Nanny . . . .'

'It's in the bag. The blue. Stop hopping around like a cat on a brick and do what you're told.'

'Can't I do it later, Nan . . . or get you one of the girls? I was just going down to the beach.'

'Sit down there, child. The beach won't run away. Don't think I don't know what's in your mind. I can't see with the lamp to knit, so I need it now before the light goes on me.'

Miranda sighed and sat down.

'You're a bully.'

'Yes. But where would you all be without me here giving you the odd little push? Dootherers.'

'I'd be down on the beach.'

'Hold that wool still, till I find the end of it. Giving cheek will win you no prizes.'

She began to wind the wool round two fingers. Her hand moving slowly backwards and forwards as she wound. Old comforting routine, thought Miranda, twitching her thumbs as the wool ran round them.

'Do you like my hair? Father didn't notice.'

10

'He notices nothing these days. The house could fall down and he wouldn't notice. Schemes. That's all is in his head. Schemes and dreams. And his old trees. Your mother had lovely hair, God rest her.'

'It's my hair I'm asking you about, Nanny. My modern hair. Do you hate it or love it? You didn't say a word when I came home yesterday.'

'I can't see why you wanted to get it cut. A woman's hair is her crowning glory.'

'Everyone's getting their hair cut. No more silly fiddling with those awful hairpins. I like it anyway. I looked at myself in the glass this morning and I thought I was someone else. Someone old.'

Nanny tweaked at the wool.

'Someone sophisticated. Do you think I look sophisticated?'

'Hold your hands out like a good girl. You're letting the wool slip.'

'I'd love to look about twenty-five.'

'People of twenty-five have a little sense.'

'I am sensible. I've spent all afternoon being sensible and dusty. Look, my fingers are all covered with ink. If I didn't do those boring accounts, who would? Answer me that.'

'Your mother was twenty-five when she came to this house.'

'We could go bankrupt, for all Father cares.'

'If she could see the state of things now she'd turn in her grave. You're as bad as the master. I don't know what the pair of you would do if old Nan wasn't here to keep things up to the mark.'

'My head is full of dust and boring figures. I want a swim, some evening air . . . .'

'Your mother had skin that was white like a lily. She didn't go rushing in and out of the sea at all hours of the night and day.'

'You're always on about the past. On and on and on.'

'Isn't it all I have now, child of grace, the memories that

11

crowd in my head. The dead.' She sighed. 'The dead.'

Miranda put out a hand and touched the old woman's knee.

'There's Father and me . . . . You have us, and you're right, what would we do without you . . . and there's Andrew. I know something you don't know about Andrew. The only thing in the whole world that you don't know.'

'Hands. Andrew? What about Andrew? He's not getting married? He wouldn't get married over there to someone we don't know.'

'He's over here. His regiment's been sent to Dublin. There's that old job done. Now can I go?'

She held the last wisp of the wool up and Nanny pulled it gently from her fingers.

'Glory be . . . wouldn't that be a great thing. Andrew coming home. After all these years. I must see to his room. I wonder if that chimney needs cleaning? Little Andrew. A great thing. I hope there isn't a smell of damp in that room of his. I tell the girls to open the window once a week, but you can't keep an eye on them all the time. Glory! Andrew.'

Miranda stood up and shook the creases from her skirt.

'I think it's terrible. Horrible.'

Nanny's hands were shaking as she pushed her needles and the wool into her bag, groped then with her right hand for the stick she had to use now when she left the house.

'Don't worry about him, pet. Didn't he come through that dreadful war? If he managed that he'll be safe as houses here.'

'He shouldn't have come. He should have refused point blank. That's what I'd have done. No, I'd have said no.'

She drew herself up into what she thought to be some military stance and said no, to a general covered in gold braid.

Nanny fiddled and fussed and talked on.

'Such nonsense you talk. Isn't he a soldier and don't soldiers have to do what they're told? Hunh? Go where they're told? Orders is orders in the army and there's no arguing agin them. It's a pity a bit of discipline didn't come your way . . . and a few others I could mention and I'll name no names.'

12

The bell of the village church, half a mile away across the fields as the crow flies, chimed out the angelus. Nanny laid her stick against the seat for a moment and blessed herself.

'Six o'clock. Oh Nanny how awful of you to keep me so long. There'll be no sun left on the beach if I don't fly.'

'Have a weenchy bit of sense.' Nanny hauled herself to her feet and clutching her bag to her chest she moved slowly over the grass towards the house. 'A weenchy bit. It's all I ask.'

There was no one there to hear her, or to answer back.

I suppose I was happy; filled with such expectations. I suppose everyone of eighteen or thereabouts is filled with expectations. No one understands then, the illusory nature of happiness. We have the same attitude to it as we do to a good job, a house, enough to eat; it is one of our rights, not the shadowy dodging thing that escapes when we need it most and then at the most unexpected moments manifests itself again for a short while. Father always seemed happy, at least when he was working among his books and maps, or discussing plantings with Mr Dillon. He was cocooned from the world by his own dreams. Like someone in a fairy tale he was hedged around by his own trees, his theories and, as Andrew would have less romantically said, his drainage schemes. He saw nothing else with the clarity he preserved for these things.

A bank of cloud was building out on the horizon, threatening the sun.

Miranda ran down the last steep slope onto the beach. The tide was curling in over the sand. The detritus of an earlier storm lay marooned quite high on the beach; bleached driftwood, tassels of brown weed and everywhere the colourless pads of dead jelly fish. Bird footmarks crossed and re-crossed near the water's edge. The oyster-catchers had

13

been catching oysters. She laughed at her thought.

'Bonsoir, Maman.'

She pulled off her shoes and walked with the decorum that her mother might have liked down to the water's edge.

'Regardez comme la mer est bleue. Regardez comme la mer est calme.'

The water that rustled round her feet was still warm.

'C'est une très belle soirée, Maman, et je vais . . . umm . . . umm . . . vous chanter une petite chanson pour vous donner plaisir au Paradis.'

She stepped from the water onto a small barnacled rock and threw her hands out in front of her, in a dramatic gesture, towards the sun.

> Au clair de la lune,
> Mon ami Pierrot.
> Prête-moi ta plume,
> Pour écrire un mot.
> Ma chandelle est morte.
> Je n'ai plus de feu.
> Ouvre-moi ta porte,
> Pour l'amour de Dieu.

'Bonsoir, chère Maman, et dormez bien au Paradis.'

'Have you gone mad or something?'

She hadn't heard Cathal's footsteps. She almost jumped out of her skin and her heart pounded inside her ribs.

'Oh golly, you frightened me. Don't do that. Out of my wits you frightened me.'

She splashed off the rock and frolicked towards him, like a young puppy.

'Hey,' he said. 'Don't wet me. Hey . . . hey . . . . Mind. I'm in my Dublin shoes.'

'I thought you weren't coming. I'd given you up. I heard the train such ages ago.'

'Nothing would stop me from coming.'

He threw his case on the sand and his hat and he stretched

his arms towards her. She stood there quite still, staring into his face, as if she had forgotten the pale city skin, the blue eyes, sparkling now with the pleasure of seeing her. 'You know that. Don't you?'

She moved almost cautiously towards him.

'You must have walked so slowly. Crawled.'

'Give me a kiss and then tell me what you were doing.'

She stood for a moment on her toes and rubbed his stubbly cheek with her soft one.

'That's not a kiss . . . .'

'I was talking to ghosts. This place is full of ghosts. You have to talk to them from time to time.'

'A French ghost?'

'No. Silly. Not a French ghost.'

She kissed his mouth.

'There! What kept you? Why didn't you run?'

'I ran all the way. I dropped in to see your father for a moment. I thought I should do that.'

She moved away from him, back into the trailing edge of the sea.

'I think you love him more than you love me.'

He sighed.

'No. Sometimes he looks so tired, but this evening he looked all up in the air . . . young, somehow . . . something . . . .'

She bent down and scooped up some water in her hands and splashed it over her face. She turned and looked at him. Drops sparkled on her face.

'Horrid journey?'

'Yes.'

The hem of her dress was wet, and clung to her bare legs. She stirred at the sea with her foot for a moment and then came back towards him. She put her arm through his and they walked together up onto the dry soft sand.

'I never know what to say when I see you first,' she said as they walked. 'I feel like a stranger, someone quite new to you. It doesn't mean . . . .'

He squeezed her arm tight against his side.

15

'I know.'

'Let's sit upon the ground and tell sad stories of the death of kings . . . unless you'd rather swim, or walk or something.'

She sat down with her back to a rock and patted the ground beside her.

He took off his coat and, folding it carefully, he slipped it between her back and the sloping stone. As he sat down he opened the wrist buttons of his shirt and with great neatness rolled the sleeves up as far as the elbows. She waited, watching the meticulous movements of his hands, until he was settled beside her, then she spoke again.

'Nothing ever happens here. The days just pass, so you begin. Tell me about Dublin.'

He wriggled his body down until he was lying stretched on the warm sand.

'You'll get sand in your hair,' she said.

'I've been trying so hard to get some work done. The exams are in two weeks. I shouldn't be here. I read all the way down in the train. I feel my eyes are going to pop out of my head.'

'You don't have to worry. You'll sail through.'

'I worry. All the time, bloody nagging worry. I want to do well for him as well as for myself.'

He put his hand over hers and let it lie, warm and light.

'You've no idea how hard it is to work up there at the moment. The atmosphere is electric. Living here you couldn't even begin to imagine what it's like . . . it's like sparks are coming out of people's heads. Everything looks normal, but when you breathe in . . . .'

Miranda pulled her hand out from under his and began to dig a hole in the sand.

'Sea weed, warm salty stones, that's what I breathe. The wind has changed. I can smell the real ocean. I haven't been able to do that for days, and look at the clouds. I think our Indian summer is going to end very soon.'

'It's not like that in Dublin. There's real anger and fear . . . even in the bloody library you can feel it. My shoulders are all stiff. It's fear. It's from staring out of the eye in the back of my

16

head the whole time.'

Her fingers burrowed under the surface of the sand; her face was quite still, almost like stone. Above them a gull drifted on the changing wind, without any apparent purpose.

'They've lifted a lot of the boys in the last few days. They seem to be getting a lot of information from somewhere. From who? That's what we all want to know. From who?'

'Whom.' She whispered the word.

The digging continued.

'You find yourself looking sideways at your friends. You feel all the time they're looking sideways at you.'

'Cathal.' Her voice was careful. 'Can't you drop it? I don't mean forever . . . just . . .'

She started on a second hole, carefully scraping the sand out and patting it into a neat wall.

'. . . till your exams are over. Give yourself a chance. Can't you?'

'You know I can't do that. I couldn't back out now. I don't want to back out.'

'Not back out. I wouldn't want you to do that either . . . but . . . well . . . give yourself a chance.'

'No. I've thought about it. Holing myself up somewhere. But I couldn't do that. I haven't the right just to look out for myself . . . not at the moment. Your father'd see that, even if you don't.'

'Father's not a fighter. He doesn't understand about fighting. He'd just want you to get on and do what you have to do.' She looked up from her digging, out across the path of the sun.

'I don't think he'd want anything to happen to you. You know what I mean.'

'Two of our lads were shot yesterday. Dead. Just walking down the road. Near the canal, minding their own business. The Tans. Bastards.'

He laughed suddenly.

'What's funny?' She asked.

'My father would say it was no more than they deserved.

Dear Mam would pray for their immortal souls and for their poor bereaved mothers, but she does that for the other lot too. Her brother was killed on the Somme. She can't see that bloody uniform as a threat. It doesn't leave much room for heroics. Does it?'

'Can't you just forget it all while you're here? Can't you think of the sun, the sea, home, us? Can't you? A few days of forgetting.'

'No.'

'I've made a tunnel. You put your hand in that side.'

He rolled over towards her and squeezed his hand into the hole. The sand was cold and damp down there and stuck to his skin. His fingers met hers.

She laughed like a delighted child who had just made a tunnel in the sand for the first time.

'Your father taught me everything. You know that; everything he would have wanted to teach Andrew.'

She looked at him for a moment when he mentioned her brother's name, but didn't say a word.

He didn't seem to notice her glance.

'We have to drive them out. They'll hang on here until we do that. They simply don't understand. I hate the thought of people being hurt too. I promise you that. I don't fight for any reason except for freedom. You understand that, don't you. You always seemed to understand. It has to be that way. It has to be war.' He pressed her fingers into the sand. 'I wish I knew how to . . . oh Miranda . . . you don't live in the real world.'

She pulled her fingers away from his, scattering the packed sand as she took her hand from the tunnel.

'There are so many different worlds. How can you say that one is more real than the other? Anyway, if you don't believe in the reality of this world, why did you come back? Why didn't you stay in Dublin?'

'You know right well why I came back. To be near you, even for a couple of days. To breathe the same unreal air as you.'

He shook the damp sand off his hand and pulled her over

towards him. She lay beside him in the comfort of his arms.

'Look how white your arms are,' she whispered. 'Look, compared to mine. You've become a real city boy. Will you ever come back, Cathal?'

He kissed her. It seemed to be the only answer that he could give.

'Blow me.'

She pushed him away as she spoke and sat up.

'You're as bad as Father. You haven't noticed my hair.'

She shook her light head in his direction.

'Indeed I did notice. You look like a city girl.'

She threw a handful of sand at him.

'A real city girl.'

'Is that good or bad? Nanny's been a bit beastly about it and Father hasn't noticed. It cost me a fortune. Do I look old?'

'As old as the Hag of Beare, but prettier.'

'I hate you.'

He put up his hand and stroked the back of her neck.

'I like that. I love that. A very beautiful thing has been revealed to the world.'

She laughed.

'I suppose you say that to the city girls too.'

'Every hour of the day.'

He scrambled to his feet and pulled her up after him.

'Let's walk a little. For days I've dreamed about walking along the beach with you. It would have been just my luck if the weather had changed before I got here.'

'We could have walked in the rain.'

'It's not the same thing at all.'

Arm in arm they set off for the end of the beach. She stretched her legs to keep pace with him. The gull flapped lazily down and took its place on the rock they had borrowed from him.

If I could be there again.

If I could change time around, I could have said, Run Cathal. Run back over the footsteps in the sand, run, run, run, because though we love you, Father and I we won't save you. You will save us and all we'll be able to do will be to remember that fact forever.

I held his warm arm close to my side and we walked to the end of the beach and as we turned to come back, the clouds were blowing up into the sky, a shivering little wind made our bare arms cold and goose pimpled. Above us, at that moment, as we turned, as my arms felt the cold wind, I saw two men on the top of the hill above us, but thought nothing of it.

'It's getting cold. When the sun starts to go these days, you really know it's autumn. How long can you stay?'

'Just the two days. I must get back to the library.'

'It's lonely when you're away. I get afraid sometimes.'

'There's nothing you should be afraid of.'

'No. You misunderstand. I get afraid for you . . . not so much that something will happen to you, but that you will do something that you'll regret forever. Something that'll change you . . . make you different, scar you in some awful way. I'd love us just to stay the way we are now, at this moment, for ever and ever.'

He stopped walking and put both his arms around her, pulled her so tight against him that she felt almost part of him. 'Silly, silly, silly child . . . .'

'I'm not a child.'

'Yes you are. A child with a woman's hair style.'

She laughed happily.

'What'll happen when you grow up, dear child? You can't stay here forever, you know.'

'I have to. You know that. There's no one else. Andrew will never come back and live here. I couldn't abandon Termon, throw it out of my life. It's been so many hundreds of years . . . . Anyway I want to live here . . . grow here. I wouldn't know what to do with myself anywhere else. This is my sanctuary. Surrounded by my ghosts. Ho ghosts! Hey ghosts! Hey, hey.'

She let go of him and ran down to the edge of the sea then, turning, embraced the bay, the world with her outspread arms. The two young men on the path turned the corner up above them and started walking down the long slope to the sand. 'I love my ghosts,' she shouted to Cathal. 'One day I'll be a ghost here too.'

He moved cautiously towards her, taking great care not to wet his Dublin shoes.

'What about me? What will happen to me? To us? Have you given any thought to that?'

'One day . . . one day we'll talk about that. When all the killing and pain is over. When we have time and freedom to think. Then we'll talk, make decisions. There'll be so much time then.'

'Miranda.'

She stood still for a moment, her head tilted to one side, listening like a bird he thought, just about to be disturbed.

She smiled at him.

'Then . . .' she repeated and the voice called again.

'Miranda.'

She laughed.

'Oh golly, more ghosts.'

She began to run along the edge of the sea, foam ruffling round her feet as she ran.

'Such an evening for ghosts.'

The words floated back to Cathal.

Two soldiers were coming down the path; he became aware of them for the first time; officers they were, their shadows trailing behind them on the pale stones of the path. Men and shadows moved down towards the beach; one of them raised his hand in the air, the shadow imitated the master.

'Miranda.'

She cut up across the sand, heading for them, running and skipping, almost dancing like a child.

Cathal stood still where he was and watched her dancing away from him. As she approached the two young men, they

21

took their caps off and stood waiting somewhat awkwardly by the rock where not so long before he and Miranda had been sitting. His coat lay there on the sand, neatly folded. The seagull had recommenced its circling. The taller of the two young men took a step towards Miranda.

'Miranda.' He held his arms out towards her and she whirled into them.

'Andrew. Brother Andrew! Oh what a superb surprise.'

'Let me look at you. Oh God, I didn't realise I'd been away so long. You've grown up. I was expecting a little girl with long, long pigtails. About so high.' He held his hand out in front of him, very close to the ground. 'Why did no one let me know? You are Miranda, aren't you? Where are your pigtails and those big silk bows? Grown up lady, where is Miranda?'

'I had my hair off yesterday. Imagine that! If you'd come twenty-four hours earlier, you'd have seen the long long pigtails. Do I really look grown up? You should have told us you were coming today. Nanny'll have your life.'

He laughed.

'She already has. We dropped our gear in the hall and she found us there. After she'd recovered from the shock I got a serious lecture about manners, but I think she was really pleased to see us. But we fled. We haven't even found Father yet. I was afraid if we stayed in the house another second she'd have us making beds, cleaning chimneys, all sorts of things like that. She said we'd find you down here. She said you were to fly up at once to her. Oh do forgive me, this is my friend Harry. Let me introduce you. Harry Harrington. Harry, this is my sister Miranda.'

Miranda let go of Andrew and stretched her hand out towards Harry.

'How do you do, Harry Harrington.'

She laughed as she spoke.

'H-how do you do.' He gave a little bow and his face went pink as he took her hand.

'Excuse me for laughing, but what a funny name you have.'

Andrew frowned at his sister.

22

'Y-yes. I suppose so. Wh-when you hear it first, it is possibly a little humorous. I think people get used to it quite quickly. I did.' He smiled.

'Were you called after your father?'

'L-luckily I was spared that. His names are Cosmo Archibald.'

She didn't say anything for a moment, but peered at his face, her head slightly forward, then she laughed.

'I don't believe you. I think you're a joker. You're more than welcome anyway, whatever your father's name may be.'

She took hold of Andrew's arm again and rubbed her face against his sleeve.

'Mind you, I do wish you weren't wearing those awful uniforms. Couldn't you have come dressed as human beings?'

'Manners sister. Remember, the plaits have gone now. You have to behave.'

His eyes wandered from her towards Cathal, who had forgotten that the tide was coming in and whose Dublin shoes had suddenly and disagreeably been filled with water.

'Won't you introduce us to your friend? Is he someone I know?'

'Silly Andrew. Cathal,' she called. 'Andrew doesn't remember you. Come and be recognised.'

Cathal, wretched about his wet feet, wondered whether to take off his shoes and his socks, and decided it was probably easier in the long run to leave them on. He squelched towards the waiting trio.

'Cathal? I don't know anyone . . . . Don't tease, Miranda . . . ?'

'Cathal,' she repeated as Cathal arrived beside them. 'Look at your shoes.'

'I'm sorry,' said Andrew. 'I've been away such a long time, I'm afraid . . . .'

Cathal held out his hand.

'I wouldn't have recognised you either. Charlie Dillon. We've all changed a bit, not just Miranda . . . . It's good to see you home again. Welcome back.'

23

He stood with his hand outstretched.

'Good Lord, old Charlie Dillon. So it is.'

Andrew looked from Cathal to Miranda, then took Cathal's hand briefly.

'Yes. This brings me back a few years all right. Still shooting, old man?'

Cathal shifted his wet feet and turned to look out to sea. Andrew addressed Harry in an explicatory way.

'Charlie and I used to play together when we were children. Mess around, you know. His father taught us both to shoot. Yes. This is my friend Captain Harrington, by the way, Charlie.'

'How do you do, Ch-charlie?'

Harry took a step towards him and held out his hand.

Cathal smiled briefly and continued to look out to sea.

'How do you do . . . sir?'

Harry put his hand in his pocket.

'And fishing. He taught us fishing too. Long time ago. I hope your father's keeping well these days?'

'He's very well, thank you.'

'And Mrs Dillon? She used to make splendid gingerbread. I hope she's well. In the trenches I used to remember your mother's gingerbread. You could tell her that.'

'I'll pass the message along. I hope you'll have time to come and visit her.'

'Do you like swimming?' Miranda took Harry by the arm and turned him around to face the sea. The sun was drowning now in the silver plucking waves.

'Oh . . . ah . . . y-y-yes. You're not still swimming, are you? It never occurred to me to bring my swimming gear with me.'

'The water here is amazingly warm. I swim right up to the end of October, sometimes even later. When the tide is right in, it's lovely. You can dive from the rocks over there.'

'I-I'd like to do that.'

'We can find you some togs tomorrow, if you like. But I think the weather's going to change. Look at those clouds.

We haven't seen a cloud for ten days.'

'Yes,' Andrew's voice could be heard, after a long silence. 'I must make a strenuous effort to get down to see your parents. This is a pretty brief visit, but tell them I'll make a strenuous effort.'

'Soon those clouds will cover the sun and we won't see it again for weeks or months . . . or perhaps ever.'

'That's perfectly horrible of you . . . just as I was all worked up about h-having a swim.'

'We can swim in the rain. That's fun. Have you ever done that? Great big drops . . . er . . . dropping on you.' She raised her voice. 'Have you ever bathed naked in the rain?'

Harry laughed. Miranda laughed cautiously.

'Miranda!'

Cathal's voice was angry.

'Cathal always gets cross when I say things like that. He thinks I'm silly. I haven't persuaded him to do it yet. He doesn't like getting into the sea at the best of times. Do you, Cathal? Except in his shoes.'

'I have to go, Miranda, my mother will be wondering what's happened to me.'

'Your shoes will be ruined. Salt water makes them go all hard.'

He bent down and picked up his coat. He shook it and little particles of sand flew around among the four of them. 'My mother'll see to them.' His voice was surly. He rolled his sleeves down and carefully fastened the buttons at the wrists before putting on his coat. Andrew stared at the sea. Miranda watched Cathal's hands again as she had watched them earlier.

'Come back tomorrow, won't you Cathal? Come to lunch. Yes. We'll have such fun tomorrow.'

'I don't think I can manage . . . .'

She put a hand on his arm.

'Please.'

He nodded.

'All right. I'll do that so.'

He moved away from them towards the rock at the bottom of the path where his hat and his bag lay. As he passed Harry, he nodded.

'Good evening, sir.'

'G-good . . . .'

'Good evening, Andrew.'

Andrew didn't look round. ' 'Evening Charlie.'

His wet shoes left heavy indentations in the sand. He picked up his hat and for some reason looked for a few moments at the inside of it before putting it on his head.

'Goodbye Cathal, see you tomorrow,' called Miranda.

He nodded again and started the long walk up the steep path.

There was a brief silence. They could hear the scrunching of the stones under his heavy feet.

'You didn't have to do that.'

Andrew hadn't moved. He still stared out to sea.

'Do what?'

'Invite the chap to lunch. After all Miranda we're only here for a . . . .'

'The first person you always asked for when you came back from school. Where's Charlie, you used to shout as you came in the door. I want to see Charlie. Why can't I go and play with Charlie? Father and I mightn't have existed, for all you cared about us.'

He kicked at the sand for a moment and then turned towards her.

'That was years ago. We were children. You were only a little brat then.'

'You were like brothers.'

'More than ten years. Everything's changed since then.'

'Not here.'

He sighed impatiently.

'You changed when you went to Winchester. I remember. You became a blinking snob.'

'I-I . . . .' attempted Harry.

'I began to grow up. That was all. After that we just had

26

different interests, he and I. Less common ground.'

'He used to bring horrid friends home to stay,' said Miranda to Harry.

He smiled.

'Like me?'

'They were not horrid.' Andrew's voice was angry. 'You were a bloody little pest.'

'You want to watch out. I still am.'

'I can see that.'

'I th-think you're right about the weather changing.'

'I just get the feeling that Charlie Dillon's got too big for his boots.'

'He's grown up too. That's all. I was wrong when I said that things haven't changed here, of course they have. People like Cathal have some sort of future now. That's good. Isn't that good? Isn't it good that people have some sort of hope now?'

He didn't answer.

'I-I think it's g-good,' said Harry to no one in particular.

'Good heavens sister, don't tell me you've become a Socialist. They keep popping up these days in all sorts of unexpected places. Tell you one thing, Mother must be turning in her grave at the thought of Charlie Dillon clomping round the house in his wet shoes. I bet he doesn't know what to do with a knife and fork.'

She took a step towards him and Harry thought for a moment that she was going to hit him.

'You need to take care what you say, Andrew. Father likes him. Remember that.'

'And you?'

There was a moment's pause.

'Yes. I like him.'

'I didn't have to ask that question. I could see it with my eyes. Making a damn fool of yourself.'

'Little b-birds in their nests should agree.'

'People like you and Father do more harm than good. Let's be nice to the natives. Let's invite them to lunch. Now, look what's happening in the country. They think they can take over. They think they know how to run the damn place; they think they can win this silly affair by shooting people who don't agree with them. If you're not careful you'll have another Russian revolution here and people like you and Father will be to blame . . . and they won't thank you for your help and encouragement, just you wait and see . . . .'

'Shut up Andrew. God, I wish you hadn't come back. You must try and understand what's happening here, and if you can't, just keep your mouth shut.'

Her eyes were starry with tears.

Harry found himself blushing again.

She took Andrew's hand and held it against her warm face.

'I'm sorry. I didn't mean to say that. I'm delighted you're home, honestly I am. Just please try and not upset Father.'

'If I thought that Father was mixed up in . . . .'

'Sssh. Don't fight with him. He's been so excited, like a little boy at the thought that you might be coming home. He'll be so happy to see you. Don't spoil it. Let's all be happy and polite to each other for a couple of days . . . like we were fourteen years ago. Please.'

She stood on her toes and kissed his cheek.

'I'll go and tell him you're here. Get him to brush his hair for a visitor. Poor Harry . . . how rude we've been. I hope you won't take the last few minutes to heart.'

Harry shook his head and watched her run across the sand. At the bottom of the path she turned and raised her hand. He raised his.

I shouldn't have come, thought Andrew. I should have had sense and listened to the voices in my head. Steer clear of Termon. The voices of sense. Stay away. Forget, forget. The common sense voices. Oh God, I thought by now I'd have been able to cope with my own emotions. His voice also in my head. Such a gentle voice he has. Son, son, son. That makes me laugh. He never said that. Fantasy voice, that one is. Son! The turbulence, the war in my brain. The moment I stepped inside the hall door I could feel the turbulence. Bloody damn house. Where is my strength?

'I s-say . . . .'

She's right. Two days. I have to play a game for two days. Then I can go. Get back to reality. Become myself, my tutored self. The self I want to be.

'Andrew?'

He heard his friend's voice.

'I'm sorry, Harry. I . . . well you know . . . I'm sorry. Not much of a welcome for you . . . a family row . . . hey?'

'Do you believe in love at first sight?'

Andrew laughed, a delighted, vigorous laugh. 'Do you believe in ghosts or fairies or life after death?'

'N-no. But . . . the most extraordinary thing has happened . . . . Maybe it's an illusion of some sort . . . . This place opens you up to i-i-ill . . . maybe we were too long in the train.' He stopped and looked almost apologetically at Andrew. 'I hope you don't mind, I think I have fallen in love with your sister.'

'Yes. An illusion.'

He laughed again and pushed his friend towards the path. 'I'm suffering from illusions too. It must be the weather. The Indian summer of illusions.'

'Miranda s-says the weather is going to change.'

'That's all right then. We can hold on to that. Only two days and then reality once more. Let's go and find ourselves some strong drink. We can survive two days of illusion if we have lots of strong drink.'

I remember that hat of Cathal's so well. It was a palish grey with a darker grey band around it; truly a city hat. He wore it dipping slightly over his right eye. I remember also, laughing the first time I saw him wearing it; he had always worn a soft brown country cap until then and I didn't think the change suited his country face at all. I got used to it though, like he would have got used to my short hair; if he'd been given the time.

In spite of the Indian summer, the evenings grew very cold, so fires had been lit.

In the hall the light flickered on the gilt picture frames, on the crossed swords, the pikes, the ornate tassels; the silver chasing on duelling pistols glittered alongside the medals in their glass-topped cases. The logs were not totally dry and an aromatic greenish smoke drifted up into the chimney. Sometimes with a crack sparks flew out and scattered burning debris that lay, bright for a moment and then dimmed, leaving tiny brown freckles on the faded patterns of the old Persian rugs.

The drawing room was bright with the light from seven or eight lamps, placed on the tables among the flowers and china and on the tall brass lampstands. The fire crackled cheerfully, but its flickering made no impression on the brightness of the room.

Miranda sat at the grand piano playing 'La Fille au Cheveux de Lin', and waiting for the gentlemen to finish their port and join her.

They sat at one end of the dining-room table, and the fire and the candles made their faces gold and soft, and the men in the gilt frames crowding the walls stared in arrogance down at them.

'What a b-bloodthirsty lot you must have been,' said Harry, indicating with a flick of his head the portraits and the paraphernalia of war that cluttered the walls.

Mr Martin laughed.

Andrew pulled the decanter over and took the stopper out.

'Father was the first Martin for three hundred years not to serve King and country. Or someone. Sometimes their loyalty was a bit dubious. Wasn't it, Father?'

'I am a farmer.' Mr Martin's voice was almost apologetic as he spoke the words in Harry's direction. 'I never had any desire for glory of that kind. I . . . ah . . . experiment a bit in land reclamation . . . that sort of thing . . . trees . . . you know . . . planting trees. I don't suppose it's very . . . . Pass your friend . . . Captain Harrington . . . the port, Andrew.'

30

'Oh no thanks sir, no port for me. It gives me a head actually. I hate to have to admit it. Jolly interesting, trees and all that.'

He caught Andrew's scowling eye on him across the table.

'Not, of course, that I know much about it . . . my p-people are very citified, I'm afraid.'

The sound of the piano reached them through the open door.

'There's so much to show you, Andrew. New land you'll never have seen before . . . reclaimed . . . a couple of hundred acres. Not just from the sea.' He turned politely to Harry. 'You must understand that one of our great problems here is wind. The hills are very desolate. You'll see tomorrow. I found that by planting thick shelter belts I was able to protect the land from the wind and gradually . . . .'

'Father . . . .'

'Yes, my boy?'

'We met Charlie Dillon on the beach.'

'Charlie . . . ah yes. A good lad. Bright. He's a great help to me in a lot of ways. I'm trying to get out a series of papers for publication . . . helps . . . yes . . . in many ways . . . sometimes as a sounding board . . . .'

'Father.'

Mr Martin looked at him for a moment.

'A good lad,' he repeated. He sighed, and then thinking better of the sigh, he turned and smiled briefly in Harry's direction. 'We don't want to bore you with . . . with domesticities, but if you're interested I can take you tomorrow and show you some of my schemes . . . and your friend of course.'

'I-I'd . . . .'

'I am a schemer. Haha. I like to think of myself as a schemer. If the weather holds. Captain . . . ah . . . .'

'Please call me Harry, sir. I'd like to see what y-you've been up to, sir. I'd be very interested, really I would. A total ignoramus of course.'

The music washed round the table, like the creeping tide.

'Do have a drink? A glass of brandy perhaps, if you won't

have port? That's good old stuff though, laid down by my father. Old. Haha. Antique you might say. It shouldn't do you any harm. It's not like the brash new stuff some people drink today.'

Harry pushed his chair back and stood up.

'If you don't mind, sir, I'll . . . . If you'll excuse me. I think . . . .' He blushed again, but in the flickering darkness no one could see. 'I'm very partial to Debussy.' Somewhat gauchely he gestured towards the door.

'Tra la lala.' Andrew, almost under his breath, sang the Wedding March.

'Run along my boy . . . Harry. Run along. Keep the girl company. She doesn't have much company. We'll follow along in a few minutes.'

They listened in silence to the sound of Harry's steps crossing the hall.

'Seems a nice chap,' said Mr Martin at last. 'There was a Harrington up at Cambridge with me. Jesus. Wonder if he's any relation?'

Between them there was only the sound of the music and the departing footsteps. Andrew twirled his glass in his fingers and frowned.

'Yes,' Mr Martin spoke at last. 'Tomorrow we'll ride out. You have no idea how exciting it is to see new land thriving. Thriving. I think even you will feel something. Such prospects open up for . . . well for . . . .'

'Miranda's grown up.'

'Oh . . . ah . . . yes. Of course. You don't notice so much when you're living all the time with someone. She's become quite a sensible young woman. She's had her hair cut.' He laughed for a moment. 'She doesn't think that I have noticed, but I have. Indeed I have. She had hair like her mother. But you wouldn't remember. Long, wavy hair. Your mother used to be able to sit on her hair when it was down. You never would have seen that.'

'The last time I was here she had a plait right down to her waist, tied with a big bow, like a butterfly. A great big

32

yellow butterfly. Of course I remember Mother's hair. I remember . . .'

'You don't notice the time flying past and all of a sudden your children are grown up and you have difficulty bending down and picking things off the floor. Yes. She's a good girl.'

Andrew poured some more port into his glass.

'Why don't you think about sending her over to London for a while? Aunt Helen would be delighted to have her. Six months or so.'

'I never could stand Helen. Even your mother would never ask her to stay.'

'She's not as bad as you always made her out to be.'

'A dreadful woman. Plain too. I always thought it strange that your mother could have such a plain sister. Maybe she's improved with age. Some women mellow.'

'I know she'd love to have Miranda.'

'I don't think Miranda would want to go.'

'Well, I think she should . . . if you want my opinion. She's at the age she should be meeting people.'

'She does meet people.'

'Father, you know what I mean.'

'You might as well finish up that port while you're at it. It will have lost its bloom tomorrow. It's a pity your friend doesn't drink it. I opened it specially for you both. Ask her if you want to, my boy, but I don't think she'll want to go.'

'If you were to insist.'

'Come now, why should I insist?' One of the candles began to flicker wildly and he leant across the table and snuffed it with his finger and thumb.

'For her own good. If Mother were alive . . . .'

Mr Martin sighed.

'I think we should spare Miranda all those things that your mother would have thought important. I can't see . . . .'

'You've always been so hopeless. Can't you look into the future? What's the future going to be here for a girl like Miranda? She should at least see a bit of the world before she becomes . . .'

33

He took a drink and then stretched out his hand towards the decanter again.

'. . . stunted. Stifled.'

'Such strange words you use,' muttered Mr Martin. 'This country is in a state of evolution and you use the words stunted and stifled. I hardly think you are being fair or looking clearly at the situation. It would seem to me, that when your country is in a state of evolution, you should be there, living through it. Otherwise something may be lost to you forever . . . lost in you . . . if you see what I mean. Maybe I'm wrong.'

'Of course you're wrong. Apart from anything else, there are areas in the country where people like us are no longer safe.'

His father laughed.

'Come come my boy. I am no threat. Whom do I threaten? I can see a future . . . .'

'Oh God! Nothing here ever changes. You can't see beyond the end of your nose and you talk about the future. You may find the future is going to be something you didn't bargain for. Mother always said . . . .'

'Let's not bring your mother into this. I know what your mother would have said and done. She wanted something for her children that I never wanted . . . and for me also. She wanted me to . . . I had to fight her off, become a schemer. Now it's my life. I have my own visions, my own freedoms. This is where I belong, no matter what may happen in the next few years, and I believe Miranda thinks the same. My roots are long and deep into this earth.'

'Romantic rubbish.'

'So are yours, my son. You should bear that in your mind.'

Stunted. He used that word. Father told me all that he had said after the whole thing was over.

Perhaps he was right.

Perhaps I have never become a whole person.

What is a whole person?

I don't remember what I saw in front of myself. I have no recollection of any sense of purpose; no search for a pattern. I was of course very young, very immature. Perhaps my problem was that I never reached maturity. I never allowed myself that luxury.

What a strange state to approach death; virgo intacta in so many ways.

Children.

I would have liked to have had children; to talk to about my dreams if nothing else.

Of course they wouldn't have listened. Children never do; but they remember later.

I remembered later. I understood my father's dream later. I saw how much closer he was to sanity than we gave him credit for.

For years after Cathal's death he and Mr Dillon drove round the countryside giving lectures, talking at public meetings; they haunted the Department of Agriculture and the various Ministers. They never let up. All through the Civil War, out and about all the time; such crazy energy they seemed to have. I used to get so frightened here on my own, worrying about the pair of them driving in the dark, blind like fools to what was happening around them.

Mr Dillon always wore the black band on his sleeve. Even after his death just before the second war. They put the band between his fingers like some people put rosary beads. I cried when I saw it there.

My father died not long after that. He was old of course, but I think he felt the loss of his one true friend. Servant, some people would have said; master and servant. But it never seemed like that to me.

They never called each other by their Christian names, that is true; nor ate formally in each other's houses. But their lives were so bound together, their dreams were the same dreams, their tragedies the same tragedies, they spoke a language to each other that none of the rest of us really understood.

35

Isn't that what love is, the discovery of a mutual language?
They are lighting the lamps now. Their shadowy figures grow
in the lamplight. They touch the coverings. Their hands
smooth my hair. I had hair like my mother's until I had it cut
off that day in Cork. Such freedom that was, such pleasurable
freedom.

Harry paused just inside the drawing-room door and looked
across the room towards Miranda. It was a while before she
became aware of his presence and then, in a certain confu-
sion, she took her hands from the keys and stood up.

'Please don't stop,' he said. 'I heard you from the dining
room. I didn't think you'd mind if I c-came in. If I l-l . . . .'

She smiled. 'No. I don't mind.'

'Go on playing then. I love Debussy.'

In spite of his words she moved away from the piano,
towards the fire.

'Do you play?'

Her dress was red, just tipping red silk shoes.

He felt his body tremble as he watched her move, watched
the dress tremble around her.

'A bit.'

She rubbed fiendishly at her fingers as if they might stiffen
suddenly on her and never work again.

'Not nearly as well as you d-do. M-my fingers don't work
any more.'

She stretched her hands out towards the fire, splaying her
fingers wide.

'It's so long since I've been able to practise. His Majesty
doesn't supply Steinways to the mess.'

She laughed and then gestured towards him, beckoning
him to her side; or to the fireside, he wasn't sure which.

'You look so nervous there, hovering in the doorway.
Come in. What are you nervous about? I won't eat you. Do I
look as if I'd eat you?'

He shook his head.

'N-n-n . . . .'

He moved cautiously towards her.

'I'm sure you'd like some coffee.'

She pulled the silk bell rope that hung beside the fireplace. In the distance he could hear the bell jangle.

'I didn't get it before. I didn't know how long you'd stay in the dining room.'

'I thought I should leave them to themselves. They m-must have so much to talk about. Anyw-way . . . .'

There was a long pause. She wondering if he was stammering and waited politely for him to continue speaking. He didn't. He looked into the fireplace and said nothing.

'Anyway what?' she asked him eventually.

'I thought I'd like to come and listen to you playing the p-piano.'

She nodded slightly in acknowledgement of his words.

'They won't you know.'

'Won't what?'

'They won't talk to one another. Not really you know. They get afraid.'

'Oh rot. What's there to be afraid of? They haven't seen each other for years.'

'They've never had anything to say to each other. They're not really very good friends you know. I'd have thought you might have gathered that. They don't have very much in common.'

'I suppose all families are like that. I don't have m-much in common with my people n-nowadays. I . . . .'

'Play. Will you play? I'd love to hear your stiff fingers.'

'I-I c-can't . . . .'

'I insist.'

She took his arm and pulled him over to the piano. 'Oh do. Please do. We've lots of music. Look! What would you like?'

She opened a box beside the piano and pulled out books and books of music and carefully written manuscript sheets.

'Chopin? Will you start off with Chopin? I'm absolutely

rotten at Chopin and I love him so much. I do him no justice at all. I clomp when I play Chopin. It's awful.'

He stood in silence determined to resist her demands until she turned and smiled up into his face.

'Please Harry. You have no idea what pleasure it would give me. Just to hear some other fingers struggling, just to hear some music.'

He blushed.

'You'll laugh.'

'Cross my heart and hope to die, I won't laugh. Even my music teacher isn't coming any more. The train was held up one day and some men were taken off it. He was terrified. He's quite absurd really. I mean to say who on earth would want to harm him? He adamantly refuses to come any more. That was six months ago. So please, please.'

'Righty ho. I'll have a stab at something. S-something easy. No Chopin.'

He began to look through the music.

'And if you l-laugh or even smile I'll stop at once. I promise.' He laid a book of Schubert Lieder to one side and Chopin's Nocturnes.

'Something very romantic. I feel peculiarily romantic tonight.'

Not Brahms; three leather-covered books with gold tooling, someone must have loved Brahms. Schumann, Schubert, he put them both to one side. He heard her voice and looked up. A young girl had come into the room with the coffee.

'Put it on the table Bridie and I'll pour it out myself. Thank you.'

'Will I fix the fire, Miss Miranda?'

'It's all right. Don't bother hanging around for us, we can manage. I've all these men to do the work for me this evening. Isn't it lovely?'

'Nanny's going wild about Mr Andrew being home. It's like God came down from heaven. We have the uniforms all sponged and pressed for him and the other young gentleman.' She nodded in a friendly way towards Harry. 'To get the smell of the train off them. The smell of them old trains is terrible.'

'Thank you very much Bridie. Don't let Nanny have you up all the night with her fussing. Be firm, that's what you have to be with Nanny, very, very firm.'

'It's easier said than done.'

The girl moved towards the door.

'Goodnight miss. Goodnight sir.'

'Goodnight.'

They both said the word at once and began to laugh as Bridie left their room.

'Have you chosen?'

He picked up a volume of Mozart piano concerts arranged for four hands.

'How about a d-duet?'

'That's not fair.'

'Let's have a go.'

He sat down and set the book up in front of him.

'Listen. This is about the most romantic piece I know.' After a moment of staring at his fingers and willing them to work, be began to play tentatively the first bars of the Andante from the piano concerto no. 21. His fingers fumbled and fluffed.

'Now please don't laugh.'

She came over and sat down beside him.

'I'm not laughing.'

He laughed for no apparent reason and then the sound strengthened and began to flow. After listening to him for a few moments, she rubbed her fingers together, pressing them hard each against the other, and then she too began to play.

Andrew moved uneasily as the sound of the music reached him; his head was thick with wine and ghostly pressures.

'I . . . .'

After the long silence his voice sounded strange in the dim room.

39

His father turned his head and looked towards him.

'My boy?'

'My mother's hair,' was all he said, his voice thick too with wine.

Mr Martin sighed.

'That was all so long ago. Over, done with. The past is better forgotten.'

The young man shook his head, the room swayed for a moment around him, and then he stretched out his hand for the decanter, the comfort of cold glass in his grip. The men on the walls smiled faintly as a log flickered; they, too, had known the room to sway.

'Are you going to get drunk?'

Mr Martin's voice was peevish.

'I may.'

'I would prefer it if you didn't.'

'I'm sure you would Father, but, as you said yourself, it would be a pity to leave the port. You don't have to sit there and watch me though, you know that. I like my own company. I get on better with the ghosts when I am on my own.'

Mr Martin pushed back his chair and stood up.

He moved slowly towards the door. He heard the clink of the glass on glass as Andrew took the stopper from the decanter. He closed the door behind him and walked slowly across the hall towards his study, his books, his safety.

Miranda clapped her hands with pleasure after they had played the last notes. The sound of the music settled into silence, then there was the clapping of her hands and a crackle from the fire.

He stared down at his fingers in surprise.

'I got through it. I never thought I would.'

'It was good. Lovely. Your fingers aren't rusty at all.'

He smiled.

'I can't explain that. Yes I can. It's this place. This . . . .

You, Miranda . . . .'

'We must play more duets.' She interrupted him quickly. 'I've hardly ever played duets . . . only with Mr Slevin . . . the master . . . I told you . . . and that was work . . . no . . . no . . . . It was much more fun playing with you.'

He nodded.

'I hope you can stay for ages.'

'No. Alas, not this time. This time we're . . . what's the word? I c-can't remember the word.'

'Skiving is what we call it here.'

'Skiving.' He smiled at the unknown word. 'But we'll come back . . . and I'll try and practise so when we play again we can make it sound like real music. I p-p-promise to practise.'

She jumped up from her chair.

'I'd forgotten the coffee. It will be cold. What a rotten hostess I am.'

He twirled round on the piano stool and watched her move across the room. He touched his fingers together to feel their reality. She stooped and picked up the large silver coffee pot from the tray.

'Do you take sugar? Cream? I have a whole box full of duets . . . all almost untouched by human hand.'

'Just a little sugar please.'

She came towards him with the coffee cup in one hand and a small silver bowl filled with sugar lumps in the other.

'You're honoured,' she said, handing him the cup. 'Nanny only lets us use these cups when there's quality for dinner. She's a terrible snob. These are the absolutely top-class quality coffee cups. Father'll be raging. He likes big common cups.'

He laughed.

'I'm glad I meet with Nanny's approval.'

She filled a cup for herself and pulled one of the armchairs round so that she was facing him.

'Perhaps Andrew told you . . . our mother was a pianist. That's why we have so much music round the place.'

'Andrew never talks about his mother. How old was he

41

when she died?'

'Nine, ten, something like that. Old enough to know her. I hardly remember her at all.'

Bonsoir Maman.

The child's voice echoed for a moment in her head. She touched the top of her coffee with a sugar lump and watched the whiteness turn brown, then she popped it into her mouth.

'What happened to her?'

She crunched the lump with pleasure, the taste bursting into her mouth as her teeth closed on it.

'Am I being too inquisitive?'

'Oh . . . no . . . . She died in some sort of hunting accident. She was a marvellous horsewoman, so they say. I mean I don't know. I only know what I've been told. I was only . . . Nanny could tell you everything.' She laughed. 'That's not true. Nanny knows everything, but she doesn't tell. If you ask her she'll shake her finger at you.' She shook her finger at him. 'And say curiosity killed the cat. That's Nanny all over. So much locked in her head. Locked . . . and she sits and knits and broods upon it all. Hour after hour. Broods. It must be terrible to be old.'

She picked another lump from the sugar bowl and dipped the edge of it, again in her coffee.

'I hope you don't find Father boring.'

'I-I . . . .'

'I know he goes on and on and on . . . well you know . . . about his trees and that. Farming, land reclamation and all that sort of thing. It's really quite interesting when you get the drift of what he's talking about. He thinks it's terribly important. Possibly he's right. I haven't made up my mind yet. I suppose I should have by now. I like to do a lot of watching before I make my mind up about things.'

She sighed.

'I think I'm probably quite boring too. They weren't a very well suited pair.'

'Who?'

'Mother and Father. You were asking me about mother,

42

weren't you?'

'Y-yes. Do go on.'

'She had friends all over the country. She used to go and stay with them. Hunting and all that sort of thing. Father never liked going away from here. He hardly ever moves . . . just to give lectures . . . or do research . . . . He goes abroad quite a bit, to meet other people with the same . . . well, not for sociable reasons. She was sociable. Very. Anyway it happened in County Wicklow, a fall, a bad fall, that's what I was told. I don't remember much. Father had to go and Nanny cried all over the place. I don't remember what I felt, I don't suppose I understood what had happened. Andrew came back from boarding school for the funeral. He had a black band sewed to the sleeve of his coat. Isn't it funny, the things you do remember? Have some more coffee?'

'No thanks.'

'It's cold. I'm sorry. Nanny says I have no social graces. She seems to think I'd have had some if Mother had been alive. I suppose one should have social graces. What do you think?'

'I think you're the most marvellous girl I've ever met.'

Miranda threw her head back and roared with unromantic laughter.

'D-don't laugh. Please don't laugh. I-I . . . .'

'Mother. I'm telling you about Mother.' She spoke the words suddenly and quite severely. 'Mother. Andrew loved her so much. He's never been able to see Father straight because of that. I think he feels that Father made Mother very unhappy. I'm not sure he ever looked properly at them both. You must understand that I may not be right; I find I'm sometimes terribly wrong in the conclusions I come to. People are so complicated, aren't they? Even if you watch quite carefully, they're hard to understand. Father's probably right . . . it's better to stick to books and theories. It's more comfortable.'

'I don't find people complicated.'

'I don't think English people are very aware somehow.'

'Aware of what?'

43

'Of people's feelings, their complications. I'm not very good at explaining myself. You see I think Father gets a bit guilty at times about not having made her life particularily happy . . . for not being the sort of person she wanted him to be. She hated his reclusive ways. He has only ever really wanted to get on with his plans. I sometimes wonder why people get married. I mean . . . . Have you got happy parents?'

He felt himself going pink in the face.

'I've never really thought about it. They seem quite pally.'

She frowned for a moment, more to herself than in his direction.

'Father has this notion that the land should be taken over by the government and parcelled out to the farmers in economic holdings. You take what you need from your holding and the rest goes into some sort of co-operative market.'

'But that's Bolshevism.'

She looked surprised.

'Is it? I don't know what you'd call it. I thought Bolshevism was something really dangerous. He gets stacks of papers from all over the world. His study is piled high with pamphlets and books and then there's all the stuff he writes himself. He speaks a lot at public meetings. I don't go with him much, I'm afraid. I find it all a bit boring. Mr Dillon goes. He always goes.'

'What . . . . ' Harry paused a moment and then continued. 'What does he th-think of this lot . . . that w-we're having trouble with?'

'He's a Republican . . . if that's what you mean, but he believes in Parliamentary democracy, not violence . . . not murder, he hates that sort of thing . . . . Time, he says, patience and time and . . . .'

'And you?'

She pulled the red silk of her dress into little folds across the top of her knee. Her hands looked strong, not like the pale fragile hands of the girls he was used to. 'I am only in the process of forming my thoughts.' Her voice was low, she spoke down towards her hands. 'I don't know very much yet about the world.'

Harry laughed.

'I think that like most Irish people I've ever met you just talk on and on about things you don't understand very well.'

Her fingers stopped moving.

'Thank you.'

'I didn't mean to be r-rude. But you seem as a race to have this capacity for turning feeling into fantasy, and then you all get so worked up about oh . . . ah . . . d-dreams. Always dreams. M-maybe I'm quite wrong. Maybe when I've been here a little longer I'll begin to understand what all the f-fuss is about.'

Miranda stood up and walked over to the fireplace.

'I feel I have the whole weight of this war tied round my heart like a stone. If I were to fall in the sea I might drown with the weight of it. I really feel that. I'd drown. Sometimes I feel I'm drowning already.'

She bent down and picked up a piece of wood which she threw onto the fire. Sparks chased each other up into the chimney. Harry laughed again, but with unease.

'War? This a w-war? My dear girl there's nothing for you to worry about. I d-don't blame you for being af-fraid. I'd be afraid too if I lived out in the wilds like this, but it . . . .'

'You misunderstand me.'

He got up and moved towards her, longing to touch her hair, or the soft shadowy nape of her neck, or even the thin bones of her shoulder just where the red silk dress seemed to weigh on them.

'I'm not afraid. I'm not much good at explaining the way I feel.'

She turned towards him and looked almost passionately up into his face.

'I do . . . I truly believe that we . . . we . . . we, as a nation, I mean, have a future of our own. We do need freedom, even if it's only, as you and Andrew think, to make a mess of things. I don't understand why everyone can't see that.

45

Freedom.'

She said the word as if it were some magic word, had some magic power. The very speaking of the word made her shiver and she clutched her hands to her shoulders as if to warm herself.

'There is some obscure morality inside me that stops me from going out with a gun and fighting.' She groaned and turned away from him again. 'I think I'm just a coward . . . a terrible coward . . . afraid of reality. That's what . . . . That's what . . . .'

She turned back and looked at him and put out a hand to touch his arm. 'I see I've shocked you. I'm sorry. The whole thing is so difficult to explain to . . . .' She was searching for the word.

'The e-enemy?' he suggested.

She burst out laughing.

'Don't be an ass. You're such a nice person. The nicest person I've met for ages . . . a guest. And I'm a hopeless hostess. I give you cold coffee, I bully you into playing the piano and now I insult you. Will you forgive me? You must admit, though, you inveigled me into this conversation, didn't you?'

'I am quite confused. At home nice, well brought up girls don't go round talking about guns and freedom.'

'I don't suppose too many of them here do either.'

He scurried away from her, back to the piano and picked up his coffee cup.

'I must say I'm glad I met you and not any of the others. I-I'll have another cup of cold coffee now if I may, p-please.' As she took the cup from him he carefully avoided touching her fingers.

'Why do you . . .?'

'Are you n-n . . .?'

They both stopped and laughed. Miranda handed him back the cup.

'Go ahead,' she said.

'Are you never afraid here?'

46

'Why should we be afraid?'

He took a sip of his coffee.

'Why?' She asked again.

'You're so unprotected here. Such terrible things have happened. Anyone could just walk in . . . like Andrew and I did . . . j-just walk in.'

The cup in his hand was fine, almost translucent bone china, very old, the gold handle had no use other than decoration.

'We mustn't quarrel. That would upset Father. He holds to the very old-fashioned belief that whoever comes into the house must be treated with impeccable courtesy.'

'Even the Shinners? If they came storming in with guns?'

She sighed.

'You and Andrew have guns in your bedroom.'

'That's n-not the same Miranda. Y-you know . . . .'

'Of course it's the same. Only you didn't storm in. You came in logically and lawfully through the hall door and one of the girls carried your cases upstairs for you. Your baths were run. Your beds will have been turned down, the curtains pulled. Nanny will have filled your beds with hot jars, just you wait and see. The guns are there. We all know that. Everyone in the house knows that. Guns like dirty boots should be left out in the yard.'

'You have an answer for everything.'

'I wish I had. You play the piano better than I do.'

He laughed. She laughed. Young happy laughter filled the room as the music had done earlier.

'You are all so unrealistic and p-probably m-mad.'

As he spoke the door opened and Mr Martin came in.

'Well, well,' he said crossing the room towards them. 'Are you throwing that word at us as a family or as a race, young man?'

'I-I . . . .'

Miranda interrupted him.

'At me Father dear, just me.'

As Mr Martin sat down by the fire Harry could see that his

47

movements were slow and careful. Stiffness in his bones, perhaps even pain; there were signs of pain in his face.

'He thinks I'm mad, but he quite likes me in spite of it.'

She poured her father some coffee and dropped one lump of sugar into the cup.

'You've been bullying him. I can see that. My daughter, Captain . . . um, ah, has been very badly brought up. What's this, child?' He protested as she handed him the cup. 'I hate my coffee in a thimble.' He took a sip.

'Cold coffee what's more.'

'You can't expect hot coffee if you spend so long in the dining room. What have you done with Andrew?'

'He seems hell-bent on getting himself drunk, so I left him to it. So you find my daughter a little mad, young man, eh?'

He handed his cup to Miranda to be refilled.

'D-disconcerting might be a better word, sir.'

'These cups were made for the tiny fingers of elegant women.' He held the cup up between his finger and thumb and drained the coffee from it in one go. 'Ladies who sip rather than drink. Tiny white fingers. We're not like that, Miranda and I, our hands are quite unsuited to such fragility. We have too much of the peasant in us.' The white porcelain glowed pink in the light from the fire. He looked for a moment as if he might crush it in his fingers, but he handed it to Miranda instead.

'Harry plays the piano. Did you hear him?' She said.

'Miranda's mother was a very fine pianist.'

'She told me.'

'She used to shut herself up in this room for hours on end and play and play. Chopin, Beethoven, Liszt, Brahms. It was her secret life. She would never play for anyone else. Brahms. She played a lot of Brahms. The whole house used to be filled at times with the sound of her music.'

Miranda put out a hand and touched his shoulder gently.

'She used to play for me, Father. I remember.'

She crossed the room and sat down at the piano. For a moment her fingers hovered over the keys and then she began to play and sing.

'There was a man lived in the moon, in the moon, in the moon.
There was a man lived in the moon,
And his name was Aiken Drum.
And he played upon a ladle . . . . Do you know it Harry?'

'Great oh . . . nursery songs . . . . Yes, yes, I remember it.'

He pulled up a chair beside her and began thumping on the bass.

' . . . a ladle, a ladle.
He played upon a ladle,
And his name was Aiken Drum.'

Laughter, and in the laughter the door opened and Andrew stood on the threshold of the room.

'Um . . . ah . . . what . . .?'

Laughter.

'His buttons . . . .'

'Yes . . . .'

'His buttons were made of . . . .'

'Why are you singing that?'

Andrew's voice was loud and angry.

Mr Martin looked up and saw him standing there.

'It's a song her mother used to sing.'

'Good cream cheese, good cream cheese, good cream cheese.
His buttons were made of good cream cheese. Don't you remember it?'

'Why, why why?'

With each word he stepped further into the room.

'As you can see your friend Harry has an aptitude for the piano.'

'And his name was Aiken Drum. You must remember, Andrew?'

Miranda spoke across her shoulder.

'He played upon a ladle, a ladle, a ladle,
He played upon a la . . . hay . . . dle,
And his name . . . .'

49

'I must admit I don't recall it myself.'

Mr Martin spoke the words softly.

'And his name was Aiken Drum.'

'She was my mother too.'

'And then . . . what then Harry?'

'H-h-is . . . .'

'My mother.'

'. . . b-britches . . .?'

'Yes. That's it. His britches were made of haggis bags. . . .'

'I was just reminding you of the fact that she was my mother too.'

He was by the fireplace now, flushed, his eyes shining in the fire light, angry eyes, staring down at his father.

'Haggis bags, haggis bags.'

'Miranda.'

'His britches were made of haggis bags,

And his name was Aiken Drum.'

'Wasn't she?'

'Wasn't who what?' asked Miranda and Harry sang bravely on.

'He played upon a ladle, a ladle, a ladle . . . .'

'She was my mother too.'

'What on earth are you talking about?'

'How would you play on a ladle?'

Harry turned round from the piano and plucked at the strings of a guitar, pizzicato plucking, his fingers pinching at the strings.

'You hardly knew her. You always say that yourself. Nor did Father know much of her, if it comes to that.' His voice was venomous. Mr Martin seemed to shrink into the shadow of his chair. Miranda continued to play. Harry, like a magician turned his guitar into a trumpet, and blew ornate sounds towards the ceiling.

'And his name was Aiken Drum.'

'For God's sake Harry, stop playing the blithering fool.'

There was a moment's silence, then Harry laughed uneasily.

'My dear chap, it's a ladle I'm playing. I'm surprised that a m-man of y-your taste and d-discernment d-d-d . . . .'

Miranda put a hand on his shoulder and stood up.

'Maybe it's you who's playing the fool.' She moved towards her brother. Her voice was low. 'Maybe you've had too much to drink. Of course she was your mother, darling. You knew and loved her. To me she's only a shadow, one of Nanny's stories.'

Harry played four sonorous chords on the piano.

'Why don't we play bridge?'

He spoke hopefully to the company, but no one paid him any heed.

Andrew was standing over his father, staring down at the figure crumpled in the chair.

'You didn't know her. You didn't try to know her. You . . .'

'B-b-bridge? I'm a whizzer at bridge. Ask Andrew.'

' . . . never bothered about me either. From the moment she died you never gave me a thought. You treated me as you had treated her.'

Mr Martin moved cautiously in his chair as if he were afraid of some physical attack from his son.

'Miranda's right . . .' he began.

'Do you play bridge, sir?'

Miranda took hold of her brother's arm and pulled gently at it, but he shook her off.

'I'm saying what I have to say, so don't paw at me, sister.'

Her eyes had become nervous with tears.

'Poker perhaps. P-p-p-p . . . .'

She turned away from Andrew and stepped towards him, the red dress rustling softly as she moved. He put out a hand towards her and she smiled. Her eyes dazzled. She didn't take his hand.

'Why do you stammer?'

She whispered the question to him.

He shook his head. He had never known. No one had ever told him.

'You were polite and kind to me, just as you were to her.

51

You never forgot my birthday . . . even in the bloody trenches your birthday greetings arrived, but if I'd fallen off a horse and broken my neck, like she did, or been blown up . . . blown up, you'd have just shrugged your shoulders and gone back to your books . . . your trees . . . your crazy dreams.'

'You speak such passionate nonsense. Wilfull nonsense. You don't . . . ' murmured Mr Martin.

'Who ever wanted to hear about your crazy dreams?'

'You've had too much to drink.'

'I can do card tricks.'

Miranda laughed.

'Can you really. I'll get a pack of cards. I absolutely love card tricks.'

'Give your brother some coffee.'

'I don't want coffee. Let's leave your father to his musty old papers and his bog men. That's what she used to say.'

'Here.' Angrily, Miranda poured some coffee into a cup and left it standing on the silver tray. 'Much good it will do you.'

She disappeared into the darkness across the room and began opening and shutting drawers.

'Bog talk. That was all you ever wanted. You never seemed to realise how she longed for company, a civilised life, intelligent conversation. All she ever had here was your eternal gabbling about drainage schemes and shelter belts. Little did she know what so much of your bog talk was about.' He ignored the coffee.

'Shoes and ships and sealing wax and cabbages and kings.'

'Just the idiotic sort of remark you used to make to her.'

Miranda reappeared into the light waving a pack of cards. 'No more argufying Andrew. We're all going to watch Harry do card tricks.'

She handed Harry the pack and settled herself on the floor at his feet, the red dress spread around her.

'I've seen all his card tricks before. He only has four.'

'There's friendship for you.'

Harry shuffled and riffled the pack like a professional.

52

'There have been so many misunderstandings in the past. I suppose I must blame myself for . . . yes . . . indeed I must . . . son . . . .'

'Sh-shuffle. You shuffle now.'

He handed the pack to Miranda. Her fingers fumbled with them.

'Do stop quibbling, you two. Father, look, pay attention. Harry's about to dazzle us with his magic.'

'You must realise how happy I was . . . when I . . . how very, very happy . . . when you and your friend . . . . It seemed to me such a joyful moment. Yes. Perhaps you are right when you say these things about me . . . .'

'I'm sorry father.'

As if to make an amend of some sort he bent down and picked the tiny cup from the tray and drained the coffee from it.

'Cold. Ugh.'

'Pick a card.'

'I just feel so battered . . . it's the only word I can use . . . battered.'

'Don't tell me, just remember it. Pop it back, right in the middle there. That's the girl.'

'I didn't mean to make her unhappy.'

'I shuffle now.'

Magician's hands, cards flying.

'No hanky panky, Harry.'

'I don't suppose you did. I don't suppose you gave it much thought.'

'Absolutely no hanky panky.'

'Battered.'

'Now, tell me a number. Any number up to fifty-two.'

'Andrew, a number. Quick. Tell him a number.'

Andrew laughed suddenly. A light and pleasant laugh.

'Don't be fooled by him sister. He has it up his sleeve. It's why his coats always have such terrible baggy sleeves.'

'A number.'

'Baggy-sleeved Harrington, he's known as in the mess.'

53

'Andrew! A number.'

'Seventeen, if you insist.'

'Righty ho.' Harry started to count the cards onto the little table beside him. 'One, two, three . . . .'

Why does Andrew have to say what he feels all the time, she thought. Why can't he let us be happy, just for two days? We could just sit here by the fire and laugh or sing round the piano. Why does he burn so much? It's so good when we're laughing.

'. . . seven, eight, nine . . . .'

The door opened and Nanny came in slowly. She closed the door behind her with great care, her old trembling hand turning the knob, clutching at it as if she might fall down if she let it go. They watched her in silence.

'The sheets are fresh from the hot press and there are jars in the beds.'

Miranda grinned up at Harry.

The old woman turned from the door and moved slowly towards them.

'Ten, eleven, twelve . . . .' Harry whispered the words, his hands moving, his eyes on the old woman.

'I wouldn't want ye to be worrying about damp.'

She looked sharply from face to face.

Hawk eyes, thought Miranda, getting the measure of us, seeing everything.

'It's well after eleven now. You shouldn't be keeping the master up so late. He's up with the lark, rain or shine and away out before breakfast looking at his old trees.'

'Fourteen . . . f-f-f-'

'He needs to get his little bit of sleep. He's not getting any younger.'

Mr Martin laughed.

'Nanny . . . .'

'And it's time you were in bed young lady.'

'Shush Nanny, shush a minute. Can't you see he's doing a trick.'

'Sixteen, seventeen. The three of clubs. Right or wrong?'

54

He waved the card triumphantly above his head.

'It's right. Absolutely right. How clever. Isn't that clever? Father, were you paying attention? Now, you must tell me how you did it.'

'Baggy sleeves,' said Andrew.

'It was magic,' said Harry. 'Total magic.'

'I suppose,' said Nanny, fixing her eyes on Harry. 'Ye do have the electricity at home?'

'Y-yes oh yes. We do indeed.'

She sighed.

'It would be great to have the electricity. I keep telling the master he should get it. Keep up with the times. No one ever listens.'

'It's not as easy as all that Nanny.' Mr Martin's voice was gentle as he spoke to her. 'We'll get it one day. I promise you that. Everyone in the country'll have it one day.'

'And poor old Nan'll not be here to see it.'

The hawk's eyes moved towards Andrew who cleared his throat uneasily. He took his empty glass from the mantelpiece.

'Well . . . yes . . . ah Nanny . . . yes. I'll just have one more drink and then I'll be off to bed.'

'You'll do no such thing.'

'We'll all go to bed. Won't we? A long day . . . .' His voice faded.

'You've had more than is good for you, my lad. I can see it in your face. Give that glass here to me.'

She held her hand out towards him. For a moment he hesitated and then like a good as gold child he put the glass into the waiting hand.

'Thank you. You'll just come up with me now and I'll see you into your bed.'

Andrew didn't move. Miranda stared up at her great-grandfather who scowled down from the wall.

Nanny's voice rose to a slightly higher pitch.

'Come along Andrew when you're told and take that impudent look off your face. March.' She pointed towards the door.

'Nanny . . . .'

'Not a word. March, I said.'

He began to move slowly across the room. She moved in behind him to cut off any retreat he might have been thinking of making.

'And you're not to go opening the windows, letting the night's fumes into your lungs. We don't want you taking sick on us. I've enough on my hands as it is.'

Near the door he faltered and looked back pleadingly at the three by the fire.

'March,' said Nanny.

He opened the door and they both marched out into the hall. There was an explosion of laughter as the door closed.

'Oh G-G-G-God. Oh marv-v-vellous . . . .'

'I'm sorry . . .' began Mr Martin after he had stopped laughing.

'The B-British army need men like her.'

'I'm . . . .'

'Don't say a word sir. He gets a bit worse for the wear from time to time. We all d-do.'

'Cold coffee or no cold coffee, I think I'll have to have another thimbleful after that.'

He started to push himself up from the chair.

'I'll do it Father. Harry . . . more for you?'

He shook his head.

'No thanks. No more for me. T-too much coffee keeps me awake.'

He shuffled the cards together and put them back in their box.

'That's an old wives' tale, if ever I heard one.'

She handed her father his cup of coffee as she spoke and then bent down and kissed him on the top of his head. He looked up at her surprised, and smiled.

'No, I assure you. After more than the smallest amount of coffee I suffer from p-palpitations, stomach c-cramps and the most g-ghastly insomnia. I lie there hour upon hour counting platoons, companies, b-battalions all crawling on their stomachs under the wire.'

He banged the box of cards against the arm of the chair, a drumbeat Miranda thought it sounded like.

'Some men whose faces I've never seen before and men who I . . . and m-men . . . and m-men . . . thousands of them . . . all going out.' He laughed suddenly. 'It's the coffee.'

'I recommend you to try counting sheep like everyone else. Just jumping neatly over a small hedge. That can be very soporific.' He put the box down on the table.

'Sheep.' He laughed again. 'Y-yes. I must try counting . . . .'

'You look so young.'

Mr Martin handed the empty cup to his daughter.

'So untouched by anything. Of course when you get to my age, everyone under forty looks young. You do look untouched.' He stood up and took a step towards Harry, searching his face for signs of tragedy. He shook his head.

'I must take my old bones to bed, or I'll have Nanny down chivvying me as well. We all have to do as we're told in this house. So, if you'll forgive me.'

Harry got to his feet politely. Mr Martin held out his hand.

'I bid you goodnight, young man. I hope you won't have too much trouble with the companies and platoons tonight.'

Harry touched the outstretched hand for a moment.

'Not here sir . . . . Not in this place.'

'You'll see to the lamps, Miranda?'

'Don't worry darling. Goodnight.'

They kissed, cheeks touched cheeks, like the French do, thought Harry.

Neither of the young people spoke as they watched him cross the room and open the door. He turned and bowed towards them.

'Sweet dreams,' said Miranda.

She moved around the room in silence, bending towards each lamp, her face glowing for a moment in the light and then disappearing into darkness as she blew out each flame. The red dress lost its brilliance as the light diminished. As she went towards the last lamp he moved over towards her.

'M-M-Miranda . . . .'

'You see,' she said, frowning down towards the light. 'You turn this little screw and then give a little blow. Here, you try.'

He fumbled with his hands, the wick flared up.

'Mind . . . .' She took control.

'I could sit and talk to you for hours.'

'Don't touch the mantel or you'll burn yourself. Goodness you people with electricity are such noodles. Here, blow now . . . blow.' Obediently, he blew and the room was in darkness save for the light from the hall that lay in a bright stripe on the floor.

She moved away from him, treading on the path of light and her dress murmured as she walked.

'Promise . . . you'll teach me your card tricks tomorrow.'

'I'll promise no such thing.'

There was one lamp left in the hall at the bottom of the stairs. The shadows of the banisters quivered on the wall. The men in their frames seemed to sleep. She bent over the lamp and her shadow engulfed the hall.

'You go on up,' she said, 'there's a lamp on the landing, you won't lose your way.'

'I'll do it. I c-can. Let me.'

Her fingers were on the screw. He felt them warm under his. Her eyes were filled with yellow light.

'Don't set the house on fire,' she said and left him. She ran up the stairs and her shadow moved too, a giant shadow. He bent and blew and the shadow disappeared. She laughed from the landing.

'Goodnight Harry. How clever you are.'

'Sweet dreams. Sweet d-d-dreams.'

How easy it is to forget that the world exists.

Of all of us Cathal was the only one who saw any reality at all.

He was perhaps the only one who knew how to love.

That sounds mad, but we were all so busy loving our notions of ourselves, that we had no energy left to offer love outside ourselves. Except maybe Harry, but then Harry never belonged here like we all did.

Harry was cool fresh air when someone leaves a window open on a hot summer day.

Harry was seduced by us, by Termon, by Ireland, I suppose, like so many people are. He saw us in radiant autumn light casting giant shadows. We were never plain, pain-filled people to him.

I never discovered about his stammer. He only smiled and shook his head when I asked him about it. Very English that, not wanting to disclose things. Maybe it's admirable.

I never could have married him.

For years he used to write me delightful letters, each one ending with the same proposal. After the first three or four I stopped refusing him, I just took it for granted that he knew I meant no, forever.

Forever.

That awful word.

Nothing is forever; not even the long beach and the rocks below the house; down the years they have taken on a new shape; old rocks here, now covered with sand, new shapes uncovered there. Today there is a deep rock pool near the bottom of the path that didn't exist all those years ago. In it small crabs scurry sideways, weed moves, acid-green fronds, sometimes the flash of a tiny fish can be seen through the reflected sky. Only the very highest tides reach it, wash it out.

No forever.

I loved Cathal and then he became a dream.

There is no one left who will dream of me.

My back aches.

Cathal's pale arms were spiked with black hairs to just above his elbows and above that the pale skin of his shoulders was smooth and soft, waiting for the summer, waiting to brown again when he came back to Termon, to the long beach and the curling waves, to me.

Up my back and out round my pale shoulders the burning fire of dying smoulders all the time.

Someone is there.

Someone is always there.

I don't need to be afraid, they say. I am not afraid, only disturbed by pain.

I suppose they shot him in the head.

We never knew.

Shattering his gaunt face, the rock-pool eyes in which I had seen my own reflection. I see that shattering sometimes in nightmares. That wasteful spilling.

Is it the pain that makes me think such thoughts?

If the pain would only go I could see again, hear the voices.

If I cry out?

Yes, then they come.

They come to my call, to the sound I make.

They know how to rearrange my bones.

In the early mornings the shadow of the hill lies dark on the beach and distorts and discolours the opaqueness of the bay with its green and grey shades and the shivering of the trees.

That morning there was still blue in the sky and clouds seemed to hang unmoving in the air. Tiny waves flickered on the horizon and white bird's wings were caught by the sun as it moved up from the east.

Cathal stood alone in the shadow of the hill; not even one bird pecked its way along the sea's edge.

Forlorn, she thought as she ran down the path.

He never turned, though he must have heard her running feet. She had to touch his shoulder before he moved.

'Statue,' she said. 'Good morning, statue.'

He turned then towards her and they threw their arms around each other and stood locked to each other, not saying a word, not kissing, not moving, each one staring into the other's reflecting eyes. Only the sea breathed and wings and waves flickered far away.

'Oh Jesus Christ, I am such a fool.'

He spoke the words after such a long time that she had almost given up hope of hearing his voice.

'A fool?'

'I thought you wouldn't come. I thought . . . .'

She took his hand and squeezed it hard against her warm morning face.

'I always come.'

'They . . . .'

'They have nothing to do with us.'

'That is too easy to say.'

'It's true. You mustn't make things complicated, Cathal. Nothing can ever make me change the way I feel.'

He smiled at her.

'All over the world people are saying that to each other. A million people at this moment are saying just those words.'

'What a horrible thought. I don't like it when you say things like that.'

'Are you going to swim?'

'A quick dash in and out. You?'

'No. I've got out of the habit. I'm staying on dry land until next summer now.'

She pulled off her dressing gown and handed it to him and ran quickly into the sea. The beach shelved quite quickly and she was swimming in a moment. She made a large circle in the water, disturbing the reflections and then came ashore again.

'Freezing,' she said taking the dressing gown from him. She put it on and then wriggled out of her togs clumsily. 'But healthy, very very healthy.' She shook her head like a dog. 'It's great having no hair. Run.' She stood on her toes and kissed him with her wet lips, a cold salty taste in his mouth.

'Run on home. I'll see you at lunch time.'

'Are you sure?'

'I'm running.'

She ran back up towards the path.

61

'Of course, I'm sure.'

As she panted up the path she waved. He turned and walked slowly along the beach, past the grey standing rocks; alone, slowly, along the long beach, back to the world.

What black bird is like that, she wondered, as she watched him, treading with such care? What long-legged black bird, his head slightly poked as if he were looking for worms in the damp sand?

As she came up towards the house and round the corner by Nanny's tree she heard a voice declaiming.

'Awake! For morning in the bowl of light

Has flung the stone that puts the stars to flight.'

Harry stood in the open window of his bedroom and his voice carried out over the lawn.

'And lo . . . .'

He bowed courteously in her direction as he spoke the word.

'L-lo the Hunter of the East has caught

The Sultan's Turret in a noose of Light.

Good morning beautiful lady.'

She waved her wet togs at him. 'How poetic you are so early in the morning.'

'I was very expensively educated. A terrible waste of money really. I c-can't remember the next line.'

She laughed.

His pyjamas were pale blue silk with dark blue piping. Most unmilitary, she thought.

'Is it early?' he asked. 'I've been standing here for ages watching the old Hunter of the East catching things. I saw you running down the path . . . to the sea? Was that where you went? Sherlock Harrington deduces you have been swimming.'

She went rather red in the face.

'I . . . .'

'Can that be good for you? It's October after all. Or am I being old-fashioned?'

'I go down to watch the birds. The beach in the early

62

morning belongs to the birds. They dance.'

'And you swim. I nearly came after you but then I thought that m-maybe . . . m . . . m . . . .'

He paused and looked at her. She was dusting the sand from her feet, stooping down, fingers flicking.

'You ran through the mist. Here one minute and gone the next. You might have been a ghost for all I knew . . . . Do you know . . .?'

He leaned dangerously out of the window towards her. She looked up at him and smiled.

'What?'

'I really expected to f-find myself tucked up in the barracks when I woke this morning. It was such a relief to find all this . . . and you . . . and there is this most romantic smell wafting . . . w-wafting . . . .'

'Smell?'

Miranda wrinkled up her nose and sniffed.

'Bacon and eggs.'

She laughed.

'What a dreadful fraud you are. Omar Khayyam and bacon and eggs don't go together at all.'

'Alas, I have to admit to being e-e-essentially a bacon and eggs m-man.'

'You're a clown. I'm cold. I must go and get dressed. I don't usually hang about after my swim.'

She moved away crunching over the gravel towards the side door of the house.

'It's nice to have a clown around the place. Hurry up and get dressed, clown, or Andrew'll have eaten all the bacon.'

'I'll just throw on some clothes, and then I'll be down.'

'Not your beastly uniform I hope.'

She was gone in through the door. He heard it close below him.

'C-casual tweeds,' he said to the air. 'I h-had thought of casual t-t-t . . . .'

Breakfast over, Mr Martin beckoned Andrew into his study. Books were scattered and piled everywhere. On three easels were large detailed maps of different parts of the estate, the new plantings carefully shaded in. Out into the bay reclaimed land and that in the process of reclamation were marked in different colours. The side of the hill between the village and the sea were well covered now by a forest of conifers. A system of dykes and drains covered the low lying fields near the sea.

Andrew looked at the maps without saying a word. Behind him at his desk Mr Martin pulled more maps from under a pile of papers and spread them out.

'I thought you'd be interested to see . . . . It's been so long . . . you haven't . . . . I've always been so bad at writing.'

'I don't really understand.'

His father came over and stood looking at the maps in front of them.

'Those ones are just showing the place in general . . . the whole place. You see that's the village and the home fields, here the land right down to the bay, and that one there is Old Termon and the hills. I have it all here in much more detail. If you're interested. Look, there, that red shading, that's all reclaimed land, several hundred acres. Dillon and I thought that system up ourselves. Look . . . .' He almost ran back to his desk.

'See. Look here . . . if you're interested. It's a sort of cross-hatching of drains. If you're interested.'

Andrew didn't move.

'We even went to Holland. Dillon and I. Spent a week there. I'm sure I must have written and told you about that. Fascinating.'

'It must have been.'

'I racked my brains and then I thought why on earth not go to Holland. Of course we made a couple of terrible mistakes but it all worked out in the end. I've written a very interesting paper . . . .'

He looked at his son in silence for a moment.

'Paper,' he repeated. 'Yes. It was published in the *Journal of Forestry and Estate Management*. Of course it is all tied in together with re-afforestation plans . . . I mean that was why they were interested. Quite a learned publication . . . I can show you . . . .'

He turned towards the book shelves behind him.

'I see you haven't changed.'

'Changed? All those pamphlets there, those are mine. You must read . . . . Why should I have changed?'

He looked worried for a moment.

'Should I have changed?'

'Times are changing.'

'Yes. Yes that's true indeed. I really feel now that my work is coming to a head. Soon very soon I will have something to offer. I need Charlie Dillon's help for a couple of weeks. He makes me keep my nose to the grindstone and then all my facts and findings, all those experiments, all gathered together . . . that's, you see where he comes in. He seems to be able to put some order into my chaos. I am in the middle now of getting my proposals down on paper.'

'What proposals?'

'It's a comprehensive scheme my boy . . . I'm not just talking about this place. I have been in the privileged position of being able to carry out my experiments here, but I'm talking about Ireland.'

He looked at his son with triumph.

'Ireland. Plans for deciduous forests and huge belts of shelter, quick-growing trees for cropping, tree farming, you've heard, I'm sure, of tree farming . . . that will be part of my scheme. You know we destroyed the land when we cut down the forests.'

'Oh come Father, isn't that a little melodramatic?'

'No. No. I'm certain of that . . . . Planting combined with major drainage schemes. Thousands and thousands of acres of derelict, abandoned land can, must be given new heart. Think of what that'll mean to the people.'

'Wild mad dreams.'

65

'No.'

'And when you have all this stuff gathered together, what are you intending to do with it?'

'Present it of course.'

Andrew laughed.

'To whom do you intend to present your opus?'

'I . . . .'

'Who the hell will care?'

'Our own government. We will have a government of our own before too long, I believe. If they care at all for the future of the country . . . the land . . . .'

'God! Father, you are an old fool. Even if you do have a government of your own they won't even begin to know what you're talking about. They'll be a bunch of jumped-up gunmen. What makes you think they'll be interested in drainage schemes?'

Mr Martin sighed.

'I think we must agree to differ in our views about this country. If you had chosen to spend more time at home . . . .'

'Home! This hasn't been my home since Mother died.'

'That was the way you seemed to want things to be.'

'You never asked me, did you? You never appeared to care.'

There was the sound of voices in the hall and Miranda's laughter.

'Did you?'

Mr Martin raised his hands in a helpless gesture.

'Andrew. Hey ho, hey ho hey.'

The door opened and Miranda put her head around.

'My goodness you both look cross,' she said. 'Come on Andrew. We've even brought your nag to the door for you. It's far too nice a day to stuff inside. I bet you've been rowing with Father. I'll tell Nanny on you.'

She disappeared, and then as she crossed the hall she called back to her father.

'By the way, I've asked Cathal to lunch. You don't have to worry, I've told Cook. Do come on Andrew. We're not going to wait all day for you.'

Andrew made no move.

'You'd better go,' said his father. 'She's right. The weather could change at any moment.'

He sat down and pulled some papers towards him, picked up his pen, bent his head, perhaps forgot his son standing there in the room.

Andrew stood for a moment watching him and then went out, closing the door quietly behind him, to join his sister.

It was strange galloping without the weight of hair around my neck.

Freedom.

I was quite sedate and they rampaged like a pair of school-children.

Freedom.

The strain left Andrew's face as we cantered along the strand.

Our faces were polished by the warm almost sultry breeze that blew from the west. We jumped low stone walls and galloped in and out of the sea making absurd patterns over the sand. We scrambled up the hillside to the ruins of Old Termon and looked back across the bay at this house, warm, secure, its chimneys streaming flags of smoke, its windows alive with sun. We skirted the edges of one of Father's new plantations, and leaving the horses munching grass we climbed across one of his dykes and walked to the sandhills facing out to the ocean.

Light and shade as the clouds moved; our faces shadowy at moments became unveiled as the sun appeared again.

Shade and light. Concealment and revelation.

Weed floated just below the surface of the sea, great acres of it, disappearing when the sun went behind a cloud and reappearing again, heavy weighted, like my hair had been just a few days before. We laughed in the light and shade, insubstantial laughter, that the wind shook away like the calling of the sea birds, forever lost.

I remember the light and shade.

They were of course late for lunch.

When they came into the dining room Mr Martin and Cathal were standing somewhat dispiritedly sipping sherry from old cut glasses.

Miranda's face was bright with pleasure and sunshine. She rushed across the room and threw her arms around her father.

'Darling Father, I'm sorry we're late. It's all my fault, I forgot about the time. We've had a marvellous ride. Cathal hello. Mea maxima culpa.'

She took two steps towards him and then stopped.

'Ttt,' muttered Mr Martin who liked his meals on time.

He moved towards the table. 'You'll have to have your sherry at the table. Cook will be in a terrible rage otherwise.'

He pulled out a chair and indicated to Harry to sit down. 'You see young man, I am at the mercy of my servants.'

Miranda laughed.

'Don't mind him. He's a demon for punctuality. Cathal, you sit there next to Andrew.'

'Have you met Andrew's friend, Charlie . . . Captain . . . ah . . .?'

'Who wants a glass of sherry?'

Andrew took the stopper from the decanter.

'Sister? Good morning Charlie. Sherry Harry?'

'We met yesterday on the beach. Good morning, or sh-should I say g-good afternoon. Sherry? Yes please.'

Cathal muttered something and sat down.

'Charlie hopes to have time to help me get all my papers in order. Ring the bell Miranda and let them know you're back. In another few weeks he'll have time to put his orderly mind to it. Yes. He has a far more orderly mind than I do. Mind you . . . .'

68

Miranda crossed the room and pulled the rope by the fireplace. In the far distance they could hear the clatter of metal on metal.

Mr Martin leaned across the table towards his son.

'. . . mind you . . . like you he tends to be a bit sceptical.'

Andrew laughed good-humouredly as he sat down.

'I'm not a bit sceptical Father. I'm totally sceptical.'

His father turned to Harry.

'I hope you enjoyed your ride. Where did they take you?'

'Over the hills and far away. Qu-quite b-b-b-'

'We put him on Topsy, just to see how he would manage her. He doesn't ride badly, for an Englishman.'

As she passed Cathal's chair she put her hand lightly on his shoulder for a moment. He turned and looked up at her, his eyes sombre.

'How many times have I told you not to be unkind to visitors?'

'Don't worry about me, sir,' said Harry. 'I can look out for myself. That's a terrible, bad-tempered little mare though. She n-nearly had me off several times.'

Miranda laughed. 'It's true. It was really funny, wasn't it Andrew.'

Andrew smiled briefly.

'She nearly had him into a whin bush . . . you should have seen his face.'

Two young girls came into the room with dishes which they put on the sideboard.

Andrew turned to Cathal.

'I gather you don't work here?'

'That's right.'

One of the girls moved round the table putting a plate in front of each person.

'I presumed you did. If I remember right you always wanted to. You used to look forward to stepping, so to speak, into your father's shoes.'

'Times have changed. You've been away a very long time. Thank you,' he said as a plate landed in front of him. 'A lot of

69

things have happened in the last few years.'

'I had noticed.' Andrew's voice was sarcastic.

'Yes,' said Cathal. His eyes flicked towards Miranda. She smiled briefly and looked down at her plate.

'So . . . if I may ask . . . what . . .?'

Cathal took up his knife and fork and attacked the food in front of him.

'I turned out to be able to read and write . . . when I put my mind to it.'

'We went to Old Termon,' said Miranda to her father.

'Ah.'

He turned towards the guest.

'They probably explained. That was where the house originally stood. A sort of fortified farmhouse. You will have seen the shell, of course. It was built to withstand marauders, but was somewhat vulnerable to winter storms. So my great-great-great-grandfather decided that the time had come for comfortable living and he built this house. Shelter. We have a modicum of shelter here.'

'If you don't work here,' continued Andrew, 'where do you work?'

'Termon.' Mr Martin raised his voice. 'Means sanctuary. It's from the Irish you know. Tearmann. That's approximately correct, isn't it Charlie? I crack my tongue on the Irish language, I'm afraid.'

Cathal smiled and nodded.

'Tearmann,' he repeated the word.

'Sanctuary,' repeated Mr Martin.

'A u-useful name to have in times like th-th-th-'

'How do you pass your time? Earn your living? If I may be so inquisitive.'

'Oh Andrew, don't be such a bore.' Miranda leant across the table towards her brother. 'He's at college of course.'

Andrew looked startled. 'Good Lord!'

Cathal gave a little laugh.

'It even surprises me sometimes.'

'You mean to say you're at Trinity?'

70

'No. The other one.'

Andrew put a piece of cauliflower into his mouth and chewed it for a moment before speaking.

'Yes. Yes of course. The National University. Yes. Your parents must be very proud of you.'

'Tell me sir, do you have any b-b-other round here?'

'Bother?'

Mr Martin looked surprised.

Cathal spoke in a low voice to Andrew, almost whispering. 'It was your father. He pushed me. He also fought a lot of battles for me. They never would have considered such a thing if he hadn't . . . .'

'You do surprise me.'

'Trouble with the Shinners, that sort of thing? You know what I mean.'

'We'll be cubbing next week. Can't you stay a few days longer? Wouldn't that be fun, Father, if they could stay a few days longer?'

'Bother.' Mr Martin frowned at the word. 'No. No bother here.'

'I j-just . . . .'

'I promise not to put you on Topsy again.'

'This is a very peaceful part of the world. Will you have some more cauliflower? Do help yourself if you will. We always help ourselves at lunchtime.'

'I'd love some more.' He pushed his chair back and stood up. 'I'm simply ravenous after all that fresh air. Miranda, can I get you some?'

She shook her head.

'Anyone else for c-c-?'

There was silence around the table.

'Just help yourself my boy.'

Harry, plate in hand, went over to the sideboard.

Andrew placed his knife and fork meticulously beside each other on his plate.

'What are you reading?'

'Philosophy,' replied Cathal.

71

There was a moment's silence, then Andrew threw back his head and laughed.

'Philosophy!'

'I'm glad it amuses you.'

'Where do you think that'll get you? A lot of damn fool words, ideas. Who needs that sort of thing? It only confuses people. Who?'

He stared into Cathal's face, but didn't give him time to answer.

'Churchmen and scholars maybe and perhaps a handful of highfalutin writers. Are you intending to enter the Church? No. I don't suppose you are. Philosophy! Hear that Harry?' He tilted his chair back and looked across the room at his friend. 'Hear that?'

Harry cleared his throat and put the lid back on the vegetable dish. He came back to the table and sat down. Miranda's face looked slightly fearful.

'Yes,' he said quietly. 'I h-hear.'

'Yes,' he said. Jokes, jokes, jokes he thought, that's what we need now.

'Tell me Charlie, what do you intend to do with your philosophy? Hey?'

'I thought I might have a stab at changing the world. It's quite useful to have a clear mind if you want to do that.'

'What makes you think the world needs changing?'

'P.H.I.L.' Harry patted some cauliflower onto his fork as he spoke the letters.

'I have my eyes. You too have eyes.'

'I think . . .,' said Miranda. She looked towards her father. He was staring out of the window.

'Tell me more about changing the world, Charlie. I'm interested. Are you inv . . . .'

'Father . . . Father . . . .'

'P.H.I.L.O.S.O.P.H.Y.'

He banged his hands on the table and the silver rattled. 'I can spell it. I was b-best in my form at spelling. Do you know . . . .'

He turned to Miranda. He reached out and took her hand and held it gently in his.

'Egypt was the last word in my spelling book, don't you think that's odd? I never could understand why. I mean, after all, it isn't the most difficult word in the world to spell, is it? E.G.Y.P.T. Simple. Even the Gyppos themselves could get that one r-r-ri . . . . Andrew, why didn't you tell me that you had a b-b-beautiful sister?'

Miranda wriggled her hand out from his fingers. Her face was red.

'B.E.A.U.T.I.F. . . .'

Cathal stood up.

'I think sir, if you'll excuse me.'

They all stared in silence at the tall figure, the lank hands dangling by his sides. Mr Martin sighed and then gestured with the stiff, white napkin that he had in his hand.

'Sit down my boy. Don't be nonsensical. You must learn . . .' he thought for a moment . . . 'learn . . . .' He dabbed at his mouth with the napkin. 'I want you young people to become friends.' He looked around the table, only Harry looked back into his eyes.

'Sit down, Charlie. Finish your lunch.'

Cathal didn't move.

'Cathal . . . .'

Miranda gestured across the table towards his chair.

'I'm sorry sir . . . .' He spoke the words very quietly.

'What's all this Cathal business anyway? His name is Charlie. Why do you call him Cathal?'

'I prefer Cathal.' Cathal spoke before Miranda could reply. 'You can call me what you want, but just remember that I prefer Cathal.' He turned to Mr Martin and gave an awkward bow, rather grotesque. 'I am sorry sir, but I really do have to go. I'm late as it is already for . . . .'

'How w-w-would you spell Cathal?'

'An appointment. I have an appointment I have to keep.'

'Charles is Cathal,' Miranda explained to her brother.

'Charles is Cathal?'

73

'In Gaelic. So sir, if you'll excuse me. I really shouldn't have . . . but . . . .' He glanced at Miranda. 'But . . . .'

'Oh God,' said Andrew. 'I might have known.'

'Run along my boy if you have to. I do believe there's an excellent pudding. It'll be a pity to miss that. But . . . .'

Cathal moved towards the door.

'You'll be back won't you? Before you return to Dublin? There are a lot . . . .'

'C.A.H.I.L.L.'

Harry looked around for approval.

Miranda laughed.

'I'll be back as soon as I can. I'm just not sure. As soon as I can.'

'C-ca-hill?'

'C.A.T.H.A.L. If you're interested.' He was gone out of the door.

Harry looked startled. 'Now who would have thought of that.'

'Cathal!'

Miranda jumped up from her chair and ran after him.

'Wait.'

She ran across the hall and caught at his arm as he stopped to open the front door.

'Don't let Andrew upset you. Cathal . . . . He's such a tease. That's all. Don't you remember? He always used to tease us. Make me cry. Don't you remember?'

He stood by the open door and the wind flickered into the house past them and stirred the rugs on the floor and even the heavy fringes on the curtains looped back in the archway between the front hall and the staircase hall.

'The wind is getting up.'

He stared out at the gathering clouds.

She pinched her fingers into his arm.

'You were able for him then.'

He smiled and touched her face gently with a finger.

'It's not Andrew. I'm able for Andrew any time. He can be so abominable, but it's not that. I shouldn't have come at all.

74

A message came . . . but I didn't want you to think . . . and then you were so late back . . . .'

'A message?'

He nodded and drew her out onto the step, into the wind, and she shivered a little.

'A message? What message?'

'I've been ordered to a meeting. There was a note waiting when I got back this morning.'

He took her hand and put it to his lips.

'What do you . . .? Why? Cathal . . . why?'

'I don't know.'

He spoke into her fingers and his fingers that held tight onto hers were trembling.

'I hope to God they're not going to shove me into an active service unit, just now with the exams . . . I'm late as it is.' He let go her hand and they stood looking at each other. A drop of rain exploded on the step beside Miranda's feet.

'It's gone,' she said. 'Oh dear, dear Cathal.'

'What's gone?'

Another drop and then two more. The steps were becoming freckled with raindrops.

'The illusion of happiness. It was here for a moment. In spite of . . . in . . . for a moment, but it's gone. You'll take care, won't you?'

'Yes. I'll take care.'

'You'll get wet. It's going to pour.'

He moved down the steps and then stopped and looked back at her.

'That Harry . . .?'

She laughed.

'He's good company for you, isn't he?'

'He's a joker. It's good to meet a joker from time to time. You have no cause to worry. I told you that this morning. I meant it. Go along now and please take care.'

He nodded.

She watched him down the steps and then trudging down the avenue. The wind pulled at the back of his coat and he had to keep his hand to his hat. The leaves on the chestnut trees were trembling; ready to fall at last.

I was thirty-nine when father died.

Yes.

It was almost evening when I came in the door. Spring cold; spring, neither day nor night. The lights were on in the room; the electricity that Nanny had pestered on and on about. The curtains were not yet pulled and the grey devouring dusk pressed on the windows.

He was sitting in his big chair by the fire, his glasses balanced comically on the end of his nose.

He had never got used to wearing glasses; never found the knack of balancing them on the bridge of his nose; they used to slip, tilt, fall askew, if he moved his head quickly in any direction.

The door creaked as I opened it and walked into the room. He looked up from the paper, his glasses as I said balanced comically on the end of his nose.

'Miranda.'

That was all.

I never knew what he was going to say to me.

Maybe he just wanted to speak my name at that last moment. We were then both surprised by death.

The paper folded neatly, as he always folded it, slithered from his hands to the floor.

I stood in the doorway, my hair wet from evening rain and watched the paper slither to the floor, listened to the sliding sound of it, listened to the echo of my name.

'It's absolutely foul out,' I said, in answer to what I thought was his greeting.

His head just nodded forward onto his chest, like an old man dropping off to sleep.

'I'll pull the curtains.'

I moved towards the window as I spoke the words into

the emptiness.

'. . . keep the cold out.'

I looked over my shoulder towards him, surprised at the emptiness of the room. The paper lay on the floor beside his right foot. A flame fluttered in the fireplace and his face trembled in golden light.

'Father . . . .'

I stopped halfway to the window. I changed direction and walked across the big room towards him. The standard lamp behind his chair had not been switched on. I put out my hand, still chilly from the open air, and pushed the switch and stood for a moment looking down at him. His silver hair was still thick. He had always been proud of that, one of his few personal vanities. Thick and straight it grew, like the vigorous hair of a young man.

I've heard it said that hair and nails continue to grow for quite a long time after death. I wonder if that's true.

I bent to kiss the thick hair and as I leaned towards him I realised, no, that's not quite the right word . . . I became very slowly aware that there was no longer a person there. I put out a hand and touched his shoulder.

'Yes, it's Miranda. It's Miranda.'

His head sagged sideways and the glasses tipped further again, clinging now somewhat pathetically to the side of his face.

I bent down and took the glasses from his face. I couldn't bear for him to look absurd at that moment.

What should I do?

I stood there with the glasses in my hand, with the flames from the fire casting living tremors onto his skin.

What did people do at such moments?

Scream?

He wouldn't have approved.

Cry?

My heart seemed to be thundering in my ears.

I threw the glasses down onto the nearby table; the table that held on it at that moment a green volume of *Trees and*

Shrubs Hardy in the British Isles, Volume Two, carefully annotated on almost every page in his tiny neat black writing, and a brown leather folder containing a lot of his own writings and his silver fountain pen, a present from Andrew the previous Christmas. The glasses clattered down among all those things, precious belongings.

I almost ran across the room and threw up the bottom half of one of the long windows.

I knew I had to do that.

The wind rattled at the window, scattering rain drops onto the floor, struggling to enter to destroy our neat equilibrium of living. I hoped against hope it wouldn't impede the flying spirit.

People will expect me to cry. I thought that. That ought to be the natural thing to do at this moment.

Dear Father.

I thought that, like the beginning of a letter that I was never going to write.

I stood by the window and the wind buffeted me and the rain spattered the floor and my feet; my cold hands, colder than he was when I touched him, hung by my side.

I thought absurd thoughts.

I thought dear Father.

I thought how Nanny would have known what to do.

She would have cried, I thought.

She was a great one for crying at the appropriate moments, but she was practical also, she would have known who to telephone, how to face this moment.

Papers rustled on the table beside him, a wisp of smoke escaped from the chimney and curled into the room and spread into the emptiness.

I will cry tomorrow, I decided.

I am alone now forever.

I will cry when we have performed the rituals.

My tears will be my private tears.

My tears for Cathal were also private tears.

Nineteen years.

At that moment by the window as his soul flew past me, I remembered the taste and heat of those other tears.

Salty taste for weeks in my mouth.

Dolour.

That's a word we don't use much any more.

A weighty word.

I felt the weight of it gathering on my shoulders.

The wind was cold on my ankles.

'I didn't know you were back.'

My heart, expecting only silence, thumped.

I turned and saw Peggy Dillon our housekeeper standing in the doorway.

'I thought I'd better have a look at the fire.'

She began to step heavily across the room.

Her shoes, shining black, creaked as she walked.

'He'd let it out and then be complaining of the cold. Why have you that window open? Miranda?'

She spoke my name sharply.

I couldn't speak. I couldn't think of words to say. My tongue seemed to be filling my mouth, no word could possibly pass the heap of it.

'Miranda! Miss Miranda! He'll catch his death with that window open.'

I hear her rattling in the coal bucket.

Such a normal sound.

But then of course so is death normal; the most normal of all happenings and the one for which we are the least prepared. She shook a shovel of coal onto the fire.

'Miranda, are you listening to me?'

She straightened up. She had rheumatic pains in her back in the winter months and her movements were quite slow. I pushed the window down.

If his spirit hadn't flown by now, I thought, it was because it had chosen to stay where it was.

'Is something the matter with you?'

'No.'

I found the word. I spoke the word.

79

'Father . . . .'

I pointed towards the chair in which he appeared to be sleeping.

Peggy looked down at him; the soft hair, the paper neatly folded on the floor by his right foot.

'He said Miranda when I came into the room . . . and then . . . I think he's dead.'

She looked across the room at me as if I were mad and then bent down towards him. She put one hand tentatively on his knee and then touched his face, something I don't suppose she had ever done in all the years she had been with us, caring for us. She straightened herself again, with obvious pain, and unconsciously wiped her fingers on her overall. She made the sign of the cross.

'God rest his soul.'

'Amen,' I said.

Dear Father . . . amen, amen. My letter was written.

'I'm sure he'll be all right,' I said.

Tears started springing from her eyes. Out of the pocket of her overall she pulled a large white handkerchief and held it tight to her face.

'Oh . . . oh . . . oh . . . .'

I ran across the room to her, clumsily dodging as I ran the little tables covered with ornaments and photographs, glad at that moment to have something to do with myself. I put my arms around her and held her tight.

'There, there Peggy. It's all right. He'll be all right. What a great way to die. Look at it like that.'

Great heaving sobs came from her.

'I did my best for him.'

'I know you did. He knew it. We . . . .'

'I never could have minded him like old Nanny, but I did my best. God forgive me if I ever said a hard word to him.'

'Don't cry Peggy. Please . . .'

'Oh . . . oh . . . oh . . . . There I was coming into the room thinking he'd have let the fire out and . . . .'

She turned from my arms and looked at him.

'Poor Joe.'

She began to cry again.

I wonder for a moment who Joe could have been and then remembered that Mr Dillon's name had been Joe. The first time I had ever heard it used had been at his funeral. Peggy was Mr Dillon's youngest sister. I took hold of her shoulders and pushed her onto the sofa.

'Sit down Peggy. I'll get you a drink. I think we should both have a drink.'

She shook her head. 'We can't sit here having drinks with him . . . with him . . . . It wouldn't be . . . . Ooooh.'

I went back to the window and pulled over the curtains; moving to the sound of her moaning from window to window, pulling and smoothing the long silk curtains.

'Are you not crying?' she asked me suddenly.

'Not at the moment. I'm trying to think what we should do.'

'It's the shock,' she said, her voice now more composed. 'I'll be over the shock in a minute or so. Shock takes us all in different ways.'

I nodded.

'I'll ring Mr Malcolm. I think that's the thing to do.'

'Shouldn't we get the poor man to his bed? He looks so uncomfortable like that.'

'No. I'll get the doctor first. He'll know what we should do and then I suppose I'd better ring the colonel. Yes.'

At the thought of Andrew, Peggy began to cry again.

I went over and put my hand on her shoulder. 'He's happy, Peggy. He'll be really happy now.'

'It brings it all back. Joe and . . . and the bad times, Charlie.'

She said the name almost defiantly, as if it were a name she had made her mind up never to say again.

'Yes,' I said and went out to the hall to telephone.

The sound of their footsteps echoed around the hall.

The sound of rain beat against the long window halfway up the stairs.

The sound of the wind battered and then, as if in apology, it sighed.

The sound of Miranda playing Schubert in the drawing room.

As the lamplight trembled, the shadows trembled.

'I've never seen so m-much military paraphernalia hanging on anyone's walls before. Quite gives me the jim-j-jams.'

Mr Martin laughed.

'I have often had the inclination to remove it all. Start again, fresh empty walls, even some of the portraits might go, but then, I feel . . . well you know it's all part of the history of the place. You can't just dispose of the past by hiding things away . . . . They were in their way all brave men. They all served with distinction . . .'

He paused and smiled slightly to himself.

' . . . either King or Country.'

'Most people say King and Country.'

'Not in Ireland my boy. Not in Ireland.'

He opened the drawing-room door and they both went in. Miranda stood up from the piano and came towards them. Even through the closed rich curtains the sound of the drumming rain could be heard.

'See there.'

As Mr Martin continued to talk he waved his hand towards the gilt-framed portrait of a soldier over the fireplace. 'That chap there. Andrew de Poer Martin . . . a fine name. The name Andrew has been in the family a long time . . . tradition . . . you know the way it is. My father was Andrew . . . .'

'Before you get too involved, Father, do let me give you both some coffee. Some hot coffee this time. Where's Andrew?'

Mr Martin shook his head impatiently.

'Coffee,' he said.

Harry grinned at her and pointed with this thumb back towards the door.

82

'De Poer is Norman of course.'

'Of c-course.'

'He raised a troop of horse from round here . . . quite a large number of men I believe and fought under Bagenal Harvey. He was hanged outside Wexford for his pains. He has that look about him don't you think . . . a sort of premonition of disaster in his face? I've always thought so anyway.'

'Probably indigestion,' said Miranda handing him his coffee.

Harry wondered whether to ask who was Bagenal Harvey, but before he could speak, Mr Martin waved his coffee cup in the direction of another picture.

'And that chap there, the one with the red face . . . he was a general in the Peninsular War. And that's my father over there. Yes. The earlier Andrew . . . or rather, I should say, one of the earlier . . . yes. He died in the Crimea. I hardly remember him. Hardly.'

'Half a league, half a league, half a league onward,' whispered Miranda. 'Into the valley of death rode the six hundred.'

'Hardly. Yes. My mother, a most remarkable woman, for her time, lived on her own here for fifty-odd years. He was always away fighting somewhere . . . then . . . well, dying.'

He swallowed the coffee from the tiny cup in one gulp.

'Yes. He died. We brought him back, of course. I think it was quite an effort. We like to take care of our dead in this country. I was the only child they ever got together long enough to make.'

He laughed and handed the cup to Miranda.

'A strong woman. She was the best landlord for miles around. Yes. I don't think you would ever meet anyone to argue with that.'

'Is there no portrait of her?'

'She hadn't the time, she always said, to sit still long enough for her portrait to be painted.'

'Theirs not to make reply,
Theirs but to do or die.

83

Theirs not to reason why
Someone had blundered.'

'I was the first son for five generations not to wear a uniform of some sort or to indulge in . . . all that useless sort of nonsense. Of course I mean nothing personal. You . . . I mean . . . . What a sad world we live in. She made me appreciate their heroism without having to feel the need to follow in their footsteps. I don't mean of course to disparage . . . . You do understand, don't you? I do find courage a very admirable attribute.'

He looked anxiously at Harry.

There was a distant rumble of thunder. Miranda shivered and clasped her hands together as if she were about to pray.

'Y-yes sir. I think I understand.'

'I used to know so much poetry. My head was full of it, when I was young. I mean about fifteen or sixteen. Now it's all slipping away. I often wonder if it matters. Am I soft in the head or something? I wouldn't like to be soft in the head.

'I look for her every day. Even after all these years. Sometimes when I come down in the morning I expect to see her sitting behind the coffee pot. I have so many questions I want to ask her. I have neither her strength nor her resolution. Maybe Miranda will be filled with resolution . . . and energy of course, that's important too . . . I don't know.

'I used to sit up in my room and learn reams of poetry. I must have learnt half the poems that were ever written. That's what it felt like anyway.'

The thunder rumbled nearer and the windows rattled nervously in their frames.

Miranda gave a little gasp.

'I'm quite foolish about thunder. I do get frightened.'

She spoke the words to no one in particular.

Harry stared at her clasped hands and longed to hold them in his.

'So, you see, Andrew is conforming to the old pattern, tradition, call it what you will. The King or Country tradition.'

84

None of them had heard Andrew coming into the room and now he was there among them, looking down at his father in his deep armchair.

'Again? Talking about me again? What are you saying about me this time?'

He swayed slightly as he spoke.

'I was just telling your friend . . . ah . . . Harry that you are following in the family tradition. I am the odd man out.'

'Yes. You are. How true.'

'The summer's over.'

Miranda spoke in a low voice to Harry. She had unclasped her hands and they lay like white birds, he thought, on the soft red silk of her dress.

'It is O-october, after all. You must remember that.'

'October,' she repeated vaguely.

Thunder rumbled again. She pressed her fingers hard together.

He watched her hands moving.

'We don't normally have s-s-summer in O-o-o . . . .'

'I've always wondered why they call it an Indian Summer. Do you know?'

He shook his head.

'You have an answer for most things. Can't you think up one for that?'

'There's no more brandy,' said Andrew loudly. 'I've looked in the sideboard. I've looked in the corner cupboard. I've sought it here, I've sought it there. There isn't any. Where do you hide the brandy, Father?'

'Don't you think you've had enough?' his father asked him mildly.

'I think I'm old enough to decide whether I want to be drunk or sober.'

Miranda jumped up from her chair and held out her hand.

'I'll get you some. Here, give me your glass.'

He bowed.

'That's a good, dear little sister.'

All three men watched her in silence as she moved from the

light into the half-dark and then out into the hall, the red flickering dress, the glass held out in front of her. As she disappeared Andrew turned abruptly to his father.

'Tell me Father . . . .'

Mr Martin bent his head to listen, moving back into the darkness of the wing chair.

'Where do you stand? I've wondered for so long. Where? What are your thoughts about this . . . rabble? Will you answer, Father? No hedging, no half-truths?'

He turned away from his father and looked down into the fire. His eyes shone almost mad in the light from the flames.

'These Republicans? I suppose you support them, hey? I get the feeling that you support them. Let me tell you something: In 1916, when they stabbed us in the back, I thought of you. I wondered then what you were thinking. Constantly I thought of you. You have no idea what those trenches were like. No one ever told people like you what those trenches were like. The best kept secret of the century. We sat there day after day, month after month waiting to die. Irishmen, Father, in case you hadn't remembered. Thousands of Irishmen as well as all those others. Waiting to die. Watching our friends die; all those deaths . . . bloody savage deaths. Actually wishing, begging God even that the next time it might be you, put an end to it.'

He stopped speaking and the room was filled with heavy silence, a tumble of rain down the chimney caused the fire to spit, a raging, sizzling spit.

'And then those bastards in Dublin had to play at being heroes and I thought of you. I thought, this will give the old man pleasure. But what about me? Is he thinking of me? Of my men, my dying thousands? Did you ever think of them? Who thinks of them now?'

Mr Martin put up a hand in the flickering light, like a policeman on point duty, thought Harry, but ineffectual.

'Oh God, I used to pray, if only they'd take me away from here and put me in charge of the heavy artillery in Dublin, I'd blow the whole damn city to smithereens and all the damn traitors and half-traitors with it. Poum.'

He smacked his right fist into the palm of his left hand.

'Perhaps even you, Father.'

The thunder was almost on top of them now.

He turned to look at his father again.

'You don't speak. You never spoke. Mother always said that. You always looked eternally bruised. I want you to speak now.'

He leant down towards him, almost threatening.

Harry got to his feet.

'Andrew old ch-ch-ch . . . .'

'None of this is your affair. I came here to exorcise old ghosts. I should have had the courage to come alone.'

'The ghosts are in your head, my son. That is where the exorcism must take place.'

Andrew shook his head.

'No.'

'We all have ghosts in our heads.'

'No.'

The thunder now seemed right over the room in which they stood. Harry glanced anxiously towards the door, worrying about Miranda.

'In every room I hear the sound of her step, her sigh. You probably never noticed her sighs. Did you?'

His father didn't speak. Harry moved uneasily. There was another crash of thunder and then he heard, he alone heard her cry out. He ran. Neither of the other two men were aware of anything except each other, not even the thunder sounded in their ears.

'The pain of her loneliness is everywhere. In this room, trapped in this room . . . . Always. I thought that now, after so long that perhaps . . . . But I knew the moment I saw the house. I remembered at that moment the way the evening sun used to burn in the windows and I knew that I would hear the sound of her playing the piano, in here, alone. Why did you make her lead her life alone? When I saw those golden eyes I knew the ghosts would be waiting.'

87

His eyes were filled with tears, the tears of a drunk man, the tears of a child, the tears of a soldier who had eluded death a thousand times.

His father stood up.

Face to face they stood by the fire.

'Golden burning eyes. Oh God, I hate it here so much.'

Face to face they stood by the fire and they couldn't speak, only stare forlornly each into the other's eyes.

'I heard y-y-y-ou. Are you all . . .?'

She crouched down gathering pieces of glass ineptly into her hand.

'It was the thunder. The lightning. Such a flash of lightning. It just . . . .' She glanced nervously towards the window. 'I got such a fright. I . . . thought . . . I broke a glass. I . . . .'

'Here. Let me do that. Your hands are shaking. You'll cut yourself.'

'I feel so stupid.'

She stood up and placed the fragments on the table. He knelt at her feet searching for the slivers in the carpet.

'I'm afraid I've spilled quite a bit of Father's brandy.'

He smiled up at her.

'Saved it from Andrew. I'm sure b-brandy's good for carpets. I've heard that somewhere. There. I think that's the lot. Lethal little slivers, aren't they?'

He put the tiny pieces on a plate. 'Don't want anyone to cut themselves.'

She looked very pale.

'You'd better have a drop yourself. You look a bit rattled.'

She shook her head.

'I'm all right now. Honestly.'

A great crack of lightning lit up the world outside the window for a second, silvered the striking rain against black trees, walls and the far hills; silvered for a moment the white face, the hands holding together the lapels of the coat; long black coat and pale face, the ghost by the gate, the figment, the imagining.

She cried out again and covered her face with her hands and the thunder rattled above the house, the windows stirred in their frames. He threw his arms around her and pulled her tight against him and she stood there her face against his shoulder, her heart thudding so that he could feel it in his body and didn't know if it were his heart or hers. The thunder faded, flickered, faded again, and then there was only the sound of the rain lashing against the windows.

'It's moving away,' he whispered.

She didn't say a thing.

'You'll be safe if you stay here in my arms like this . . . quite, quite safe.'

She disentangled herself from his arms and moved slightly away from him.

'It wasn't just the lightning. I thought I saw . . . out there . . . .' She glanced towards the window and quickly away again. 'Out there . . . a man. Standing out there by the gate. That was what . . . . That really frightened me.'

He went over to the window and peered out at the sheeting rain.

'You can see nothing,' he said. 'N-nothing . . . . No one in their right mind would be out on a night like this.'

'I thought I saw a man. A long black coat and a . . . .'

'One of your ghosts?' he suggested.

She shook her head.

'A man. You pour out Andrew's brandy, just in case I drop another glass. Have some yourself.'

'Maybe just a drop.'

The thunder growled again.

'Here, give me your hand. Let me hold your hand. Then you will be a-a-bsolutely safe. I am immune to lightning.'

'Pour out the brandy and don't be silly.'

She turned her back on the window and perched herself on the table.

'M-M-M-iranda . . . .'

'Pour out the brandy, Harry, please.'

He picked up the decanter and a glass and moved slowly towards her. A flicker of lightning, almost friendly, skimmed around the room.

'Such a strange thing has happened to me. I'd like you to let me tell you. Please.'

'No. I don't want you to tell me anything.'

She slipped down from the table and moved away from him, away from the windows, towards the safety of the hall.

'I'd just like us to be friends. Stay friends. I'd value that more than anything. I don't have many friends.'

'Don't go. D-d-d—'

She turned and smiled at him.

'No, Harry, I'd just love a friend . . . . Can't you try and understand that?'

'I'll pour the brandy.'

She watched as he poured quite a dollop into his glass.

He held the glass up towards her.

'I'll drink to . . . h-h-hope. Will you let me drink to hope?'

'I'll let you drink to whatever you want.'

He drank.

'To hope.'

She smiled at last.

'And Ireland. I think you should drink to Ireland.'

'Your Ireland?'

'Certainly.'

She moved to his side.

'Give me a sip from your glass. I'll drink to my Ireland. I hope you will too.'

She took the glass from his hand and tasted a drop of the brandy, grimaced slightly and handed the glass back to him.

'I don't know whether I should. A-after all, why am I here?'

'You tell me why. I'd like to know that too.'

'The CO ordered me to come. It's as simple as that. I've been trained s-since the age of eight to obey orders. Like Andrew. H-h-honour the King and keep your power dry. Don't shoot till you see the whites of their eyes. Land of h-hope and gl-gl-gl — a whole lot of things like that. Things that seemed important. Ever since I went to school. I have been saturated in that kind of thinking. The nobility of war and the British way of life. I don't understand about Ireland, truly I don't Miranda, but you'll have to believe that I think we're here to help. I don't try to understand. That's not my j-j-job. I'm a clown who obeys orders.'

She laughed.

'What a speech.'

She put the glass back into his hand.

'Then clown, drink to my Ireland. That's an order. The Ireland you don't understand. Maybe if you stay here long enough we, or someone anyway, will be able to explain it to you.'

He held the glass up in the air.

'Amen,' he said.

Andrew spoke suddenly, breaking the long silence between them. The thunder now was only a murmur somewhere in the distance.

'It's so strange.'

He moved away from his father and stood for a moment by the piano looking down as he spoke at the keyboard, then paced on around the room, unable to settle anywhere.

'I died a thousand deaths in the damn war. Each one was as fearful . . . fearful.' He looked briefly towards his father as he repeated the word almost as if he thought Mr Martin might misinterpret it, '. . . as the first. I was exposed night and day to my own fear; a most humiliating experience I can assure you.'

His father began to speak, but Andrew held up a forbidding hand.

'Cowardice I suppose you could call it; that terror of dying, of pain, a feeling of disintegration inside my own head. To begin with I felt shamed by my own fear, but finally as the years went by I became hardened by it. I became a good soldier. I came through alive. I am alive. But here . . . this place . . . I am unnerved all over again. I feel the disintegration very close at hand. The ghosts, Father.'

His fingers plucked at the silk tassel hanging from the curtain's edge, pulled at the soft strands.

'I don't want to be like you.'

His father laughed.

'I long to keep my energy intact. Where the hell is Miranda? Drink keeps things quiet inside you. You don't speak?'

'What is there to say? I don't have to excuse myself to you, defend my character in any way. I have my dreams. They have never been reprehensible.'

'Dreams! What use are dreams? They merely confuse people.'

His perambulation over, he came back to the fire and stood there fidgeting now with the china ornaments on the mantelpiece.

'What is the Sistine Chapel but the realisation of one man's dream?'

'Oh come Father . . . .'

'I don't credit myself with such noble dreams, but I have longed for so many years to see this defeated country rising from its knees. I dream of seeing the land, the actual land, soil, earth treated with enlightenment . . . burgeoning, serving us all . . . .'

'Romantic rubbish . . . and you know it. Order is what mother always longed for and you would never listen. Order is all important.'

'I will never live to see the trees grow.'

'What is all this mumbo jumbo about trees and the holy bloody land? You are prepared to allow disorder to take over and you excuse yourself by talking about dreams. Build your paradise if you wish and all the people will do is spit in your face.'

'That's a risk we all have to take.'

92

'Disorder, violence, death. Look around.'

His father moved uncomfortably in his chair and sighed.

'I deplore violence. Deplore.'

'Deplore.' Andrew repeated the word with contempt.

Miranda ran into the room followed more sedately by Harry.

'Dear Father, I broke a glass. A good glass. I'm sorry.'

She bent down beside his chair and took his hand in hers.

'It was the lightning. I'm so, so sorry. It was clumsy and idiotic of me. I got such a fright.'

'She always hated thunder.'

Andrew took the glass that Harry was presenting to him and held it up under his nose before tasting it.

'I don't suppose you'd remember.'

Miranda wondered if he were addressing her or their father. She held his fingers tight. Bony fingers, not a spare pick of flesh on them.

'She used to pull the curtains tight and sit in the middle of the room, her fingers knotted together. White knuckles. She prayed, silent words, no sounds, just silent words. It is the only irrational thing I remember about her.'

He took a drink from his glass. No one spoke.

'I remember.' Mr Martin spoke after a long time.

Miranda patted his hand and smiled up at her brother.

'I don't remember. Not anything like that. How could I?'

'I used to sit beside her. She didn't want me to say anything, just be there beside her until the storm had passed. Then she would open the curtains and the day would go on.'

He took another drink.

'I used to worry about her after I went to boarding school. Who minded her when there were storms? Silly really. Wasn't it, Mother?'

He spoke to the air. He spoke to her as if she were there listening with care to his words.

Miranda let go of her father's fingers and got up.

'You're as bad as Nanny, going on and on about the past. I don't want to hear about the past any more. I want to play billiards. Come on Harry.'

She almost danced towards him, red dress swinging, and took him by the arm.

'There's so little time for fun. Let's have fun. Don't be broody Andrew. Come and play billiards. You can play Harry and the winner can play me and we won't get to bed till all hours.'

'Billiards isn't a game for women, sister.'

He smiled though and moved towards the door.

Harry squeezed her arm tight against him.

'I think it's a sp-splendid idea. I look forward to beating both of you.'

Miranda laughed.

'Not a hope. I'm really good. Amn't I Father? Will you come and watch.'

'No, no my dear. I'll just have another drink by the fire and then I'm off to bed. Sitting up till all hours doesn't appeal to me any more. I warn you both though, don't laugh too hard at her. If that scallawag says she'll beat you, she'll beat you.'

'Not a hope. When my hand and eye are steady I am unbeatable.' He took his sister's other arm. 'Even Harry's not too bad. We might put a bit of money on it.'

They went out laughing.

I always liked to hear laughter.

That was Harry's great attraction. He made everyone laugh. I suppose he must have been like that in the war too, sitting in the trenches making people laugh.

Poor Harry.

How silly to say poor Harry.

Poor Andrew would be much more to the point. He was so afraid of all the things he didn't quite understand, of dreams, disturbing ideas. He wanted to see nothing for the future, only the steep ladder he had to climb for his own success. He truly believed in the importance of success, but the past troubled him constantly. It never seemed to occur to him that Mother's unhappiness could have been to a large extent of her own making.

I wouldn't excuse Father for his inattention towards her, but I do believe he cared. He just didn't have time for the frills of a relationship. Andrew was too young when she died to recognise that. Father became the evil demon of some fairy story to him.

It makes me laugh a little.

I mustn't laugh.

My pain comes when I laugh.

They become disturbed.

I don't want to disturb them. They misinterpret the signs.

Poor Andrew.

In spite of his success, his marriage, his charming children who will sell this place when I have finished with it, he was quite lost.

He spoke all those words with such apparent conviction.

Order. Discipline. Obedience.

Such hard words, all of them.

Frightened words and frightening words.

Poor Andrew.

Held together with string.

'Let me into your head Andrew.' I said it once to him.

War-battered London was outside the window.

I was glad that Father hadn't lived to see such foolishness happen again in the world.

Trees in Hyde Park were beginning to bud with spring, grey war-streaked houses were unkempt and cold, even with the spring sun.

He said nothing.

He was just in the door that moment from the War Office in his pinstriped suit and his Brigade of Guards tie.

He stood beside me in the drawing room and said nothing. You could still smell war in the streets; dereliction and destruction held a smell that lingered for years. Flowers were beginning to grow through the dead houses. Maybe that will happen here. There it was a temporary phenomenon; here it will be permanent.

'Just for a moment.'

A child was skipping below on the pavement, crossing the rope and uncrossing it, counting to herself. I could hear the tap of the rope on the ground, but she must have been wearing soft shoes because her feet made no sound.

He came across the room to where I was standing and closed the window down.

'This room is freezing.'

His voice was irritable.

'I saw you coming up the road, marching up the road. You do march you know.'

He laughed.

'Why not, sister?'

'Well, I saw you marching, left, right, left right and then I thought . . . I'd like to get into Andrew's head.'

'Better stay out of it.'

We moved from the window towards the miserable fire, slatey coal that spat and smouldered.

'That's rotten coal,' I said. 'Can't you get better coal than that?'

'After all, there's been a war. We have to take what we can get.'

We never talked.

Never moved towards each other.

'When you retire . . . .'

He laughed.

'Old generals never retire, they only fade away. We'll meet that bridge when we come to it.'

He didn't come to it. A motor accident took care of that bridge for him.

That was some sort of luck I suppose; like Father, he didn't have to wait for death.

'I just wondered if you'd feel like coming home at some stage? You know . . . I've minded the place well, but perhaps . . .?'

'Home?'

'Yes. Termon,' I said in case he misunderstood me in some way.

He scratched at his little fair moustache before replying.

'Don't worry.'

'I'm not worrying. I just want to know would you think of coming home.'

'Nothing is further from my mind.'

'There's no need to be pompous and rude about it.'

'I – My life has always been here. It's such a stupid question to ask me. Nothing is further from my mind.'

He walked back towards the window and stood staring out across the road at the park.

'Nothing. You should know how I feel about things. I wish you . . . .'

He still fought with his moustache.

'I do wish you'd leave me alone, Miranda.'

'I only asked you a civil question for God's sake.'

'No.'

'What do you mean no?'

'I mean no to your civil question. No to Termon. No to Ireland. No, no, no. Now, will you leave me alone?'

'Yes.'

He turned away from the window and bowed ironically in my direction.

I remember that ironic bow so well. His hair was still fair and thick.

I remembered Father's hair.

Even sleeked as it was and cut to sit neatly under his absurd bowler hat, I could recognise that hair.

He held out a hand towards me and we walked towards each other in the chilly smokey room. I took his hand, cold from the street and held it for a moment against my warm cheek. Neither of us spoke.

I think that somewhere among the misunderstandings and the ghosts and the fear there was love.

Will you reject me, God, for not exploring the possibilities

97

of love?

Maybe my self-imposed solitude was a sin?

It is so hard to tell whether we make the right decisions or the wrong ones.

I thought of You.

Yes, You, I'm speaking to You, God and of course to Cathal. I have to keep speaking to him. Neither of you have the grace to answer me.

I have to answer my questions for myself.

I thought there was no other way to repay . . . what a mean little word . . . repay; clinking of coins and rustling notes.

Repay is rubbish.

Words are so elusive at times.

Align my life with his death; that's dry, but more what I meant to do.

Offer up my solitude.

I would truly hate to be rejected for that God.

Don't frighten me now so close to death.

Would this not be an appropriate time for comfort?

A sign?

A word?

You're not like that, are You?

You've never given signs.

You wait.

I can wait too.

They come, quickly and quietly, the ministers, administers I should say, with their needles and their soothing words. Dimming shapes.

My players now have more reality.

Mr Martin's head nodded forward onto his chest, an ageing man nodding off to sleep. The glass in his hand tilted danger-ously. A hand reached out and took the glass gently. The cold hand touching the warm skin awakened the dozing man.

'Oh,' he said, startled by the cold hand against his warm

skin. He looked up. Cathal stood above him, water running from his hair, his face, his clothes, making lakes on the floor around his feet.

'I wasn't asleep. I . . . .' He struggled to collect his thoughts.

'I was just . . . I wasn't . . . I must have dropped off. You startled me.'

'I saved your drink.'

'Thank you. Thank you.'

Mr Martin got to his feet.

'Charlie.'

'Yes.'

'How did you . . . well just arrive like this . . . just . . . . How did you get in?'

He retrieved the glass from Cathal's hand.

'As usual. Through the door. You ought to lock your doors. I've been meaning to tell you that for a long time.'

'I've never known that door to be locked. Never.'

'It might be wise. Now.'

'Wisdom doesn't seem to be one of my strong points. I like to think of this house unlocked, welcoming, truly a sanctuary.' He laughed. 'The fools' sanctuary.'

His eyes seemed to focus on Cathal for the first time.

'My dear chap, you're soaking. Take off your coat. My goodness yes . . . your shoes if you so wish. Throw it down there on the floor. I've never seen . . . . You're soaked through, right through to the skin.'

He bent and threw some more wood onto the dying fire.

'That'll blaze up in a few moments. You must have been out in the very worst of the storm. Let me get you a glass of whiskey? That'll warm you up a bit.'

'I won't have a drink thanks. Not tonight.'

'Take off your jacket too, don't stand on any ceremony.'

Cathal shook his head, shivered and held his hands out towards the fire.

'Is something the matter?'

Cathal stood silently looking down into the fireplace where

the flames were beginning to grow, once more around the fresh wood.

'Sure you won't have a drink?'

'Positive.'

'Well sit down then. Pull that chair up to the fire.'

Cathal didn't move.

'I shouldn't be here at all,' he said at last.

'Can I help you in any way? You're in some sort of trouble. I can see that.'

'No. Yes. Trouble. Yes, trouble. Listen to me . . . you've got to get the two soldiers out of the house and away. Soon. Tonight. Soon.'

'The two . . . oh yes . . . I'm afraid I don't understand.'

'Orders have come.'

'Orders?'

'Yes. Orders. Don't waste time. I have wasted too much time already, foolishly standing out there in the storm. Just get them away.'

'What do you mean, orders? Whose orders?'

'Can't you guess? They are to be shot. Executed. Assassinated. Call it what you like. One word's as good as another. Gunmen will be arriving here before daylight. In their beds. Taken by surprise.'

'There must be some mistake.'

'That was the way it was supposed to happen. They have been under sentence ever since they arrived in Dublin. They're working for British Intelligence.'

'I . . . .'

'There is no mistake. Believe me.'

'Charlie . . . .'

'For God's sake look at the thing straight. Andrew isn't a schoolboy any longer home for the holidays, as he used to be. He's an officer in the British army. He's the enemy. You know as well as I do, we are a country at war.'

Mr Martin sighed.

'I've never been able to understand why people need to kill each other.'

Two of Cathal's fingers had gone dead and numb with the cold. He began rubbing at them with a sort of fury.

'This isn't the time to be working it out. Sometimes it's necessary . . . that's what they say. That's what I would have said . . . in order to survive . . . in order for freedom to survive . . . in order for sanity to survive. I'm as bad as you are for talking. Lookit . . . what I'm saying is true. Will you go and get them . . . get them away to hell out of this.'

'There isn't a man round here, Charlie, would shoot my son. I'm sure of that.'

'Amn't I trying to tell you, it's from Dublin they're coming. They know nothing about you or your son only that they believe he's dangerous. The dangerous enemy. They won't be talking when they come. They won't be asking any questions. My orders are . . . my orders are to show them the . . . to make the way easy for them. To . . . . My orders . . . .'

'That's enough. I have been blind.' He moved across the room as he spoke and poured a large glass of whiskey and carried it back to Cathal.

'Here. Drink this. You'll catch your death of cold without something warming in you. I am blind. Drink.'

Obediently Cathal raised the glass to his lips and drank.

'Four o'clock. I was to have the gates open for them at four o'clock, and the hall door.' He laughed. 'The bloody hall door. It never occurred to them they only had to turn the handle. I didn't tell them that.'

'What can I say . . .?'

'I know what they'll say . . . . Informer, traitor, a lot of very unpleasant words. I never saw myself in this sort of situation, everything has always seemed so . . . well . . . straightforward. It always seemed to me to be a just war. Don't say a word. I know you don't believe a war can ever be just, but there we must beg to differ. You've never asked me about this. I feel such gratitude for that. You never put me in the position where I had to justify myself to you. I . . . .'

Mr Martin put his hand on Cathal's sodden shoulder.

'You don't have to justify yourself to me now either.'

101

'I have to talk. I feel diseased, plague-ridden in some way. I stood out there in that rain for hours trying to get up the courage to come in through the hall door. I swear I didn't know what I was going to say until I saw you there, asleep, about to drop your bloody glass on the floor. You looked so tired. You're getting on, you know. You should lock your hall door. If I hadn't been able to get in here and see you sleeping there I would have gone home. I would have let things take their course.'

'I still don't know what to say. Thank you seems miserably inappropriate . . . .'

'Let's just get the pair of them out of here, then we can speechify all we want.'

The door opened and Miranda came in.

'I thought you were going to bed, Father.' Her voice was scolding. 'Oh Cathal. It was you I . . . .' She stopped in the middle of the room and looked at them both. 'What is it? What's the matter?'

She moved again, quickly towards them, the red dress fluttering out and then clinging round her legs. She took hold of Cathal's arm.

'You're soaking. It was you . . . it . . . Father what is the matter?'

Mr Martin hesitated.

'Tell her,' commanded Cathal.

Mr Martin cleared his throat before he spoke, putting off the moment.

'Ah . . . ah . . . Charlie here says that men are coming to get Andrew.'

Miranda looked puzzled.

'Get? Who? What do you mean get?'

'Shoot,' said Cathal. 'He doesn't like to use the word. Dead.'

'Andrew?'

Miranda's fingers gripped tight into his arm.

'And his friend.'

'Is this true? Father?' She moved beside him, stared into his evasive eyes. 'Father?'

'I'm afraid so. Yes it would seem to be true all right.'

A surge of energy seemed to take hold of her, shaking every part of her body.

'What on earth are you both standing here for? Why aren't you doing something? How utterly hopeless you both are. Go and bring round the motor, Cathal. I'll go and get the others. Luckily they're still up.'

The two men stood rooted to the floor, staring at her. She stamped her foot.

'Move for heaven's sake. Move.'

Mr Martin took a couple of steps towards the door.

'I'll get the motor.' He looked apologetically back towards Cathal. 'Sometimes you know, she's difficult to start. There's a knack you have to have. A flick of the wrist at the crucial . . .'

'Father!'

'Yes, yes my dear I'm on my way.'

He almost hurried out of the room and they stood in silence for a moment listening to the sound of his feet tapping across the hall.

'He's mobilised. Now tell me . . . quick . . . . What is all this about?'

'I saw you in the dining room. I . . . .'

'You're as bad as he is. This is no time for conversations of that kind.'

'He put his arms around you. You let him . . . .'

'It was nothing.'

She stood close by him and put her arms around his neck.

'I was so frightened. Please, you hold me too, just for a moment. I am more frightened now. This isn't like the thunder. Please.' They clung to each other and she felt the damp of his clothes creeping through her red dress to her skin.

'I'm frightened too Miranda.' He whispered the words into the softness of her bare neck. 'I've done the most terrible thing.'

'I don't know what you've done, but I know . . . we know

Father and I that you could never do anything terrible. Cathal. Cathal.' Locked together they stood and the fire flickered, mellowing the air around them.

'I must go.'

He stepped away from her.

'I'd better go.'

'No.'

A wail like a peacock.

'Please. No.'

She grabbed hold of his arm.

'Please don't go. Stay here with us. Me. You must stay. I couldn't bear to think of you out there on your own. Cathal, Cathal. Cathal, please don't go away.'

'I'll stay.'

She sighed with relief.

'Good. Is that a promise? You won't slip away when my back is turned, will you?'

He shook his head.

'I'll stay.'

'I'll go and get the boys. Tell them.'

She ran out of the room.

Cathal slowly paced from the fireplace to a window, to another window, past the big round table loaded with flowers and books and photographs in silver frames to the fireplace again and then back to the long sweeping gold silk curtains and over to the piano. His feet were like lead, his head, his heart like lead. The piano keys were lit by a silver lamp on a tall stand. He began to pick out a tune, that never seemed to quite make sense, as his finger stumbled along the keys.

All around my hat I'll wear a green coloured ribbono.
All around my . . . .

'I sup-p-ose it's too much to ask what's going on?'

Cathal was startled by Harry's voice. He quickly lifted his hand from the piano.

'Miranda has some garbled story. I g-g-ather we have to

leave in a h-h-h . . . .'

'That's right.'

The two young men stared at each other across the furniture.

'As you see,' Cathal's voice was almost conversational, 'I can't play the piano. I can't even get one finger to play the piano.'

'You're at the back of all this, aren't you?'

'Schubert, Beethoven, Chopin . . . . They're all just names to me. I can't begin to fathom all those absurd little squiggles on those lines. So many books full of absurd squiggles.'

'Andrew's ranting and raving like a lunatic in the billiard room. I was winning too. M-Miranda . . . .'

'Miranda can play the piano like an angel, can't she? I presume she's played for you.'

'I suppose I should get my gear together.'

'Has she?'

'She seemed to be indicating that we should leave in a h-h- . . . .'

'Or hasn't she?'

'Yes, she has. As you say, she plays like an angel.'

Cathal turned back to the piano and let his fingers play a few random discordant chords.

'I wonder . . .'

'I'm bl-bl-bloody wondering too.'

' . . . if that sort of thing is important.'

'What on earth are you talking about?'

'Did you learn when you were a child?'

'The p-p – Oh yes. Five or six. Maybe younger. My father had a theory that we should learn to read music at the same time that we learnt to read words. Batty idea really . . . well, that's what most people would think . . . but to give the old man his due, it wasn't a bad idea at all. I can read an orchestral score and hear the whole thing in my head. Pretty amazing, wouldn't you say? There aren't too many people can do that. People who aren't professional musicians, I mean of course.'

'I suppose not.'

'I wish to God I had the technical ability to go with it. Or a spot of genius. I can tell you I wouldn't be in the a-ar – ar . . . but I haven't either, not an inkling. I strum.'

'Strum?'

'I'm not a patch on Miranda. Mind you, I'm very out of practice. Rusty fingers and all that. There is something serious up, isn't there?'

'Yes.'

Harry nodded.

'And I'd be right in thinking that you're at the back of it?'

'In a somewhat oblique way.'

A sharp explosion outside the window made them jump. It was followed by a series of quick rat-tat-rat-tat-tats.

'Wh – wh-wh . . .!'

Cathal slammed his fingers down impatiently on the piano keys.

'Oh sweet Jesus. It's the bloody car. He's . . . .'

'Here.' Harry almost shouted the word at him. 'Watch that piano. It's a Steinway.'

'At this moment I don't give a damn what it is.'

Harry stroked the ebony case with care, almost as if it were a beloved dog.

'You have to hand it to the Germans when it comes to pianos. N-n-no one can touch them.'

'How do you stand with motors?'

'Motors?'

'If you know anything at all about them, I'd say you might be needed.'

Mr Martin almost rushed into the room, wiping his hands as he came on his white handkerchief.

'I got her going.' He spoke in the direction of the two young men. 'Mind you, I thought I was going to manage, I didn't want to get poor Paddy out of his bed at this time of the night. He's really the only person who can manage her when she's being temperamental. I get so impatient.'

He examined the state of his handkerchief and then shoved it into the pocket of his dinner jacket.

106

'Impatient. Yes. Anyway I got her going finally. It's the fine adjustments you have to make before you swing. We got as far as the front steps and then . . . .' He waved his oily hands in the air . . . 'alas . . . alas.'

'She became temperamental again?' Harry's voice was sympathetic.

'Bang . . . she went bang. Didn't you hear her?'

'Yes,' said Cathal. 'We heard her.'

'There was a lot of smoke, I'm afraid. That's not a good sign. . . . I'll have to go and waken Paddy after all. There'll be a bit of a delay, but it can't be helped. Paddy'll have her right before too long.'

'If I might h-help, sir? I'm actually quite handy with the combustion engine.'

'A man of many parts,' said Cathal aloud but to himself.

'Now, that's really very good of you. She's not old or anything like that. Only two years. She's just a bit tempermental at times. A Delage. Do you know anything about the internal workings of a Delage?'

'Just lead me to her. I'll have her going in a jiffy.'

They moved towards the door.

'My parents have a Delage. You know I wanted to go into the Royal Engineers, but they wouldn't hear of it. Not quite you know . . . you know . . . .'

His voice floated back from the hall.

Cathal rubbed at his face with his hands. He could hear steps, movements everywhere, voices calling, the door slamming and the rain interminably flooding down from the sky. When he took his hands from in front of his aching eyes Miranda was standing in the doorway looking at him. She had pulled on a long black cardigan over her red dress and it seemed to cast a grey exhausted shadow up over her face.

'Andrew has gone up to change into his uniform.'

She just stood there in the doorway, like a statue, her hands forlorn by her sides.

'What on earth for?'

'He says he's not going to be chased round County Cork in

his evening clothes by a bunch of gangsters. He's raging, Cathal.'

She took a tentative step into the room as if it weren't her room, her house even at all.

'He's had quite a lot to drink and it doesn't make him very reasonable. At first he wanted to stay here and shoot it out, but I . . . persuaded him how foolish that would be. So he's agreed to go.'

'Your father can't get the motor to start.'

'He never can. We'll have to get poor Paddy out of bed. He always says he can, but he never can. He's too impatient with it.'

'No need to disturb Paddy. Your admirer . . . .'

'Cathal . . . .'

'Your piano-playing admirer is dealing with the matter. He says he's a genius with the combustion engine. Did you know he could read music before he could walk.'

In spite of herself she laughed.

'That'll be all right then. I have great confidence in Harry.'

She stood looking at him uncertainly. The blue eyes very bright in her pale face. Her hands were no longer still, they twitched painfully at the front of the cardigan.

'You?'

She asked the question very quietly. Her voice only just louder than a whisper.

He shook his head, not wanting to answer.

'What will happen to you? We haven't begun to think about you. I . . . we . . . Cathal? Don't just stand there. What will happen?'

'What do you think will happen?'

She took another step towards him, just the one, the dress swinging for a moment.

'They couldn't do that? Why would they do . . . ? You've done so much for them. They know . . . .'

He turned his head away and looked at the fireplace. The fire was burning bravely now.

'Nobody likes informers.'

108

'But you're not . . . .'

'Nobody's going to stop and think what I am or what I'm not. I'm in the movement. I've had my orders. I've reneged. It's all very simple.'

Cautiously, almost like a child playing a game, she took another couple of steps towards him.

'But . . . .'

'There are no buts. I can't bloody well work out why I did it. I can't stand your brother or what he's fighting for . . . . It would be no skin off my nose if they were to shoot him . . . and his helpful friend. But I couldn't leave it at that. I couldn't get on with my job. Say nothing. Let the boys get on with theirs. Who would ever have known? Some bloody nonsense had to creep in.'

'It isn't nonsense . . . .'

'Perhaps nonsense is the wrong word. Weakness might be better. No vision seeker should have a place in his mind for scruples . . . or goodwill come to that. That's pathetic corruption.' He put his hands up to his face again and stood for a moment in silence. 'You're lost the moment you forget that the end justifies the means. Lost. It all seemed so easy up there in Dublin. I had it all worked out. I thought I had the courage of my convictions. We all felt the same way. We had such pride in what we were doing, in each other. God.' His voice rose. 'Where am I now? I still know who my enemies are . . . but where's pride? Where's hope now?'

She ran the last few steps to him and threw her arms around his, holding him as tight as she could against herself.

'Stop it Cathal. Stop it this minute. You can't fall apart on us now. Everything'll be all right when we get the boys out of the house. We'll hide you here . . . . We'll explain to them . . . . After a few days . . . . After a while . . . . It'll be all right. We'll explain.' Her voice had little conviction.

'How can I explain to them what I can't explain to myself?' He unloosened her hands from behind him and held them in his own.

'It's all right love, don't be upset. I'll pull myself together.'

Andrew, dressed in his uniform, came in the door. He looked at the two of them for a moment before speaking.

'Before I set out on this idiotic journey, I need a cup of coffee. I looked in the kitchen, sister, but there's no one there.'

She disentangled her fingers from Cathal's.

'There isn't usually anyone in the kitchen at this hour of the night. I'll make you some coffee.'

'Large, black, with lots of sugar. My head is full of vapours.'

'You shouldn't drink so much.'

'Coffee, not advice, is what is needed.'

A smile glimmered on her face as she walked past him.

'I'll be as quick as I can.'

'So,' said Andrew, as the last of her skirt flicked through the door. 'Round one to philosopher Dillon. I must say you look remarkably glum about it. By the way, what's your rank in the rebel forces, just so that I may address you correctly.'

'I'm a Commandant in the Irish Republican Army.'

Andrew laughed delightedly.

'What a splendid rank. Straight from the Foreign Legion.'

There was a long silence.

'I'm glad you've decided to go,' said Cathal at last.

'A strategic withdrawal old chap. I can assure you, we'll be back.'

'I have no doubt of that. With the whole damn army behind you. A sledgehammer to crush a mouse.'

'Perhaps. If it's a nasty foundation-nibbling mouse, a sledgehammer is quick and effective.'

'You're too late you know. The mice have done their work already. You don't have a few untrained rebels to crush any longer, you have a nation.'

'My dear chap, you misunderstand us. We don't want to crush you. You're all such emotional hotheads, you never stop and think, work things out. If you hadn't raised the national temperature by that ridiculous affair in 1916, the whole thing would have been settled by now. You'd have had

110

your Home Rule and we'd all be friends. That's what you wanted, wasn't it . . . . Freedom? What the hell is freedom anyway? You're a philosopher, give it a thought sometime. It's just one of those words guaranteed to make men reach for their guns.'

'Someone who has never known the lack of it is unaware of its importance.'

'You have to live by rules, disciplines.'

'Every nation has to have the right to create its own rules and disciplines.'

Andrew laughed.

'All your lot will do is fiddle around with what we've taught you. Make compromises. Believe me you'll come screaming to us for help when things go wrong. You'll cheat. Just you wait and see.'

'Why do you treat us with such contempt?'

'It's all you deserve.'

'Your father doesn't think so.'

'My father's a foolish, rather boring old man. He's passed all his life in a dream, a fantasy of trees and drains; he's never really thought about people; about how people behave or think or . . . hurt. Yes. He knows nothing about politics, don't be fooled into thinking that he does. He just wants everyone to settle down and plant trees. Paradise will exist on this earth, if we all plant enough trees.'

'I don't think you know what you're talking about.'

Andrew laughed.

'I know all right. Oh, I dare say he was nice enough to you. He encouraged you, listened to you, talked to you even; gave you some sort of confidence that you didn't have before. He's probably even paying your way through college, eh? Is he doing that?'

Almost imperceptibly Cathal nodded.

'Just another of his experiments. Look upon yourself as just another tree or perhaps a drainage scheme.'

Into the silence between them came the sound of a roar from the motor engine; it died into silence again.

'Let me mention one thing, Charlie Dillon. It's my money he spends on his experiments; my inheritance draining into his bogs and trees . . . and you.'

'Remind me to thank you sometime.'

'And Miranda's. Her inheritance too.'

'Don't let's bring Miranda into this.'

'You needn't think I haven't noticed the attention you pay to one another.'

He walked over to the window and twitched back the curtain. He looked out and down, peering to see the car. All he could see were the shining drops spattering the window-pane.

'Bloody rain,' he said, then turned back to look again towards Cathal.

'Perhaps that's the way your aspirations lie. You see yourself possibly as a country gentleman? Your just deserts no doubt after centuries of slavery. Sitting in my father's chair at the dining-room table . . . and Miranda. I'll tell you one thing, Master Commandant, I think I'll see you dead first.'

'We used to be friends.'

'We used to be children.'

The car coughed alive again and Harry's voice shouted something.

'Yes.'

'In those days there was nothing in our heads but swimming and ponies and climbing trees.'

'You used to call for me when you came home from school. Remember Miranda said that? Where's Charlie? Remember that. I remember the sound of your voice in our kitchen. I used to wait for you to come . . . to run down to our house. I had no better friend.'

'Summer friends.'

'I used to wonder what it was like in your boarding school. Did they slam you when you didn't know your work, like they slammed us? Did you sleep in a room with long rows of hard, narrow, beds? Did you cry at night because you were lonely? I never asked you any of those questions. I was lonely for you

112

when you were away. Did that ever occur to you? Not just summer friends. Do you remember we used to go with the men to cut the Christmas tree? Do you remember the dust flying out from under the saw, that ripling crash as the tree came down? That was always such a day wasn't it? And your mother used to send me up the witch hazel tree to get the first flowers, that was just before Christmas, wasn't it?'

Andrew laughed suddenly. 'Do you remember the night we escaped out to try and catch the badger down in the wood by the stream? The blackness of it. It was the first time I'd been out in such blackness.'

'You were bitten. I remember the yells of you.'

'Yes. There was the most terrible row next morning. I got blood all over the sheets. I've still got that scar on my finger. Look.'

He held his hand out towards Cathal, his first finger pointing. Cathal moved closer and looked at it.

A pale tracery patterned the skin near the top joint. Tentatively Cathal touched it.

'Imagine that now, after all these years.'

'Your mother.' Andrew spoke softly. 'Surely your mother's not happy about . . . .' He waved the scarred hand for a second and then let it drop to his side.

'They know nothing about me. About what I do. We're not that great with each other since I went to college. We don't really have the same interests any more, no talking points beyond family matters. I don't have to tell them what I do with my time. They're good people.'

'Yes.'

'Good people. There's a lot of things they don't understand.'

'Charlie . . . I asked them not to send me over here. You needn't believe me if you don't want to.'

'But you're here.'

'Yes.'

'That's what matters. That's why they want rid of you.'

'Yes.'

Miranda materialised beside them with two steaming cups of coffee. She handed one to Andrew and then turned to Cathal. 'I made one for you too Cathal. I thought you might be needing one.'

'Thanks.'

Andrew took a sip. Hot and sweet as he had asked for.

'I hate this place. It's like a bloody quicksand. I have to fight all the time to save my . . . I don't know, integrity sounds too grand a word to use. I don't want to be like him. In forty years' time, I still want to have energy and hope and place. Believe me, Miranda, in forty years' time there'll be no place for us here.'

'Of course there'll be place. I will be here in Termon. I will have place, my place, our place.'

He shook his head.

'No. You'll have compromised yourselves out of existence. You and people like you and Father will never have the guts or the energy to stand up and demand your rights. You'll shut your eyes to what is happening. You'll acquiesce. Acquiescent people. Then one day, you won't exist any more. Maybe the country'll be better off without you. I don't know. I won't know. I won't be here to see. I want to exist. Once this war is over, I'm never coming back here again.'

The engine coughed and then throbbed and then continued, a deep healthy sound.

'The Englishman has saved the day,' said Cathal.

Two rich growling honks sounded.

'I knew he'd do it,' said Miranda.

'Good old salt of the earth Harry.' Andrew clapped his hands in ironic salutation.

They heard the hall door open and the wind scurrying through the hall followed by Mr Martin and Harry.

'The chap's a genius,' called Mr Martin from the hall.

As he came into the room he scattered patterns of rain around him on the floor. 'Knows more about it than Paddy. I told him he should start up a garage. He'd make a fortune. Listen.'

The car panted gently outside.

Harry followed him into the room looking modest and oily.

'Good old Harry,' repeated Andrew. 'Perhaps we should go now, before the damn thing stops again.'

'I'll just w-wash . . . I'll pop upstairs and w-w-w . . . . The great drawback to the combustion engine is the oil. I'll collect my toothbrush as well. I never feel safe travelling without my t-t-toothbrush.'

'Get a move on.'

'I've wakened Paddy. I thought it the best thing to do,' said Mr Martin. 'He'll drive you to Cork. He knows the road like the back of his hand. You'll make sure he gets something to eat once you're there?'

'Of course. I presume he's reliable.'

'Paddy! Of course.'

Andrew sighed.

'I also presume you wouldn't know if he were or not.'

'Paddy's reliable,' said Cathal.

Andrew nodded thanks in his direction.

'I don't know what to say about all this,' said Mr Martin, taking off his dripping coat and slinging it over the back of a chair. Miranda picked it up and shook it and carried it out into the hall.

'There's no need to say anything.'

'It's all most unfortunate . . . ah . . . most . . . .'

She laid the wet coat over one of the hall chairs, half-listening to their voices and half to Harry's steps on the stairs and across the hall. He carried a small case in one hand.

'Clean hands and a toothbrush. I've left some of my gear up there in the hopes we'll be coming back. Will you invite us back?'

Inside the room Cathal moved uneasily towards the window.

'They've done their homework very well, Father. I have to give them that. I am a sort of glorified spy. I can't say I like the role very much.'

His father merely waved his hands in the air.

115

In the hall Harry caught hold of her hand.

'Miranda.'

She wriggled her fingers, but this time he held fast onto them.

'You know,' said Andrew, 'when I get away from all this . . . this . . . I think I'll study the techniques of armoured warfare. Those tanks are pretty amazing, Father. Men galloping across the countryside in tanks. That will be the warfare of the future. Or airplanes of course, but the thought of being a knight in a tank appeals to me very much.'

Cathal plucked the curtains apart for a moment. The rain was slacking off. He could see Paddy clambering into the driving seat of the car.

'Why don't we run away and get married?'

Harry held her hand tight so that she couldn't escape.

She laughed.

'Why do you always laugh at me?'

'Because you're always joking . . . I presume you're joking?'

'N-n-no.'

They looked at each other.

Mr Martin and Andrew were suddenly in the doorway looking at them also.

'This time, I'm quite serious,' said Harry.

'We're not really very well acquainted.'

'Does that matter? We have fifty years or so to get acquainted.'

Miranda pulled her hand away from his.

'I'm sorry . . . oh Harry. I never know when you're being serious . . . I'm sorry.'

Andrew put a hand on his friend's shoulder.

'She's saying no, Harry, I'm afraid.'

'No?'

'I'm sorry,' she repeated. Her voice was gentle. 'I'm really very sorry, dear Harry.'

'You can hear my heart splintering inside me. Listen.'

Honk. Honk. Honk.

116

The three young people laughed nervously as the horn sounded. Miranda took Harry's arm and propelled him towards the door.

'I'm sure the young ladies in Cork are very good at mending broken hearts.'

'F-fractured ones perhaps. Mine is in tiny pieces.'

'Dear nice Harry, you are a most comfortable person. I have been so happy to have met you. We are going to be good friends, remember that.'

The car was waiting, Paddy at the wheel muffled against the rain and wind. The rain sparkled in the headlights.

'We're not saying goodbye you know. I've left lots of my g-g-gear up in my room.'

'No. We're not saying goodbye.'

Mr Martin was at their side.

'Come along, my boy, let me introduce you to Paddy. With the pair of you in the motor, you should have no trouble getting to Cork. Indeed you could probably travel the world if you so wished. He also has your touch.'

'Father, don't go out in the rain without your coat.'

He paid no heed to her and hurried down the steps.

Harry took her hand and kissed it gently.

'M-M-M —'

'Go on you dear silly thing.'

She pushed him out into the dark and stood watching from the doorway.

Andrew had stepped back into the drawing room. Cathal was standing still staring out of the crack in the curtains.

'She should marry a gentleman. She'll be wasted on you.'

Cathal turned and looked at him.

'Possibly.'

'Tell me, when you get your so-called freedom, what then?'

'There will be no more killing. We will build.'

'What a simple soul you are.'

Cathal said nothing.

'God. . . I'd give anything for a drop of whiskey.'

Cathal put his hand into his pocket and pulled out a silver

hip flask.

'Here.' He moved over towards Andrew. 'Take this with you. It might come in handy on the journey.'

Andrew took the flask. It seemed full.

'Thanks. A real boy scout, prepared for any eventuality.'

He looked at the flask, turned it over in his hand, felt the weight, the smoothness of it.

'A nice piece of silver.'

'Your father gave it to me. He said every soldier needed a hip flask. You'd better keep it. I seem to have failed somewhat in my duties as a soldier.'

Andrew unscrewed the top and took a quick drink.

'A temporary loan,' he wiped at his mouth with the back of his hand. 'Until we meet again.' He pushed the flask into the pocket of his greatcoat. 'Philosopher Dillon.'

He made a gesture with his hand that was part salute, part wave.

'Goodbye Andrew . . . or perhaps I should say slăn.'

'Would I appear too ignorant if I were to ask . . .?'

'Be safe. After all you might as well be safe.'

'I'll be safe all right. I wouldn't like to guarantee your safety though. The insecure deal very unkindly with those they believe have betrayed them.'

Cathal neither spoke nor moved.

'Come with us, Charlie. It's the only sensible thing to do.'

Cathal smiled.

'Sense,' was all he said.

'Andrew!'

Miranda's voice called to him from the hall.

'I'm on the side of sense,' said Andrew. 'For better or for worse. Coming.' He patted the flask in his pocket.

'Yes,' said Cathal.

'You're sure you won't come?'

'Yes.'

'In that case, I'm afraid I have to say adieu.'

He touched Cathal lightly on the shoulder and left the room.

'Cathal,' he said as he went.

'Thank you,' said Cathal.

Andrew's feet marched across the hall. Voices called, the car revved and then more voices called. It could have been any day, any time, any people saying goodbye. The car roared for a moment and then stuttered off down the avenue.

Father looked so old at that moment. He took a step back into the lighted hall and his face looked ready for death, filled with a terrible resignation that I had never seen before.

'Will I lock the door?'

I had to ask the question twice before he shook his head and laughed.

I hear his laughter now echoing in the hollow hall of my skull.

Why do we laugh when we should cry?

Here.

Is it only here in this sad island?

I suppose we might drown God with our tears.

Swim, swim old bearded man. Keep your nose above the water.

Why do you allow us to torment ourselves the way we do?

There are no answers.

We always ask the wrong questions.

I always ask the wrong questions.

I.I.I.

'What use is a locked door?'

That was his question.

He walked through the hollow hall into the drawing room. His frame was stooped with all those years of leaning over books, searching for answers to his own questions.

He stood for a moment looking at Cathal. The distance across the room between them seemed enormous.

I watched.

I breathed so softly at that moment so that no one might

hear that I was there.

He walked across the room and stood by Cathal and then slowly put his arms around Cathal's shoulders and kissed him on each cheek.

I had never before seen men embrace.

Cathal stood within the embrace and then put a hand up to touch my father's cheek.

They never spoke a word.

Then my father moved away and, bending down, threw some wood on the fire.

'What should we do now, Miranda? What do you think we should do?'

Mr Martin stood up.

The fire crackled.

Miranda came towards them.

'Wait, I suppose. There's not much else we can do, is there? Cathal and you and I? We'll just wait.'

'Quite.'

He sat down in his armchair.

'We'll wait here until daylight comes. Things never seem so bad in the daylight. If – well – if nothing – no one – '

He paused and seemed to search for acceptable words and then sighed.

'We'll be able to think more clearly in the daylight. We could sleep a little if need be. Here in this room, the three of us. I've always loved this room. My mother loved this room. I remember she had a palm tree in here for a time, over in that corner. Yes. One's mind functions better in the daylight. I've often wondered why that should be.' He steepled his fingers and stared over them at the fire in silence for a moment. He coughed, almost apologetically, and then spoke again.

'Just one thing. If the need arises, I will do the talking. Please both of you, young people, leave the talking to me.'

'No one will listen,' said Cathal. 'Your kindness, your

goodwill are no defence against their weapons. That's all we have . . . people like us . . .' he smiled ironically as he used the phrase ' . . . bloody goodwill.'

He dug his hand into the pocket of his trousers and pulled out a gun. Miranda gave a little gasp as she saw it in his hand.

'There.'

He emptied the magazine and threw the gun and bullets onto the table.

'No more guns. Amen.'

Mr Martin appeared not to notice.

'I will do the talking none the less. No matter what you may think. It seems to me to be the only thing to do. Meanwhile, as we sit here waiting for the morning, perhaps Miranda could play us something on the piano. A little Bach perhaps, my dear? It's a long time since you've played any Bach for me.'

'No,' said Cathal.

He took Miranda's hand in his and led her to the sofa.

'She's going to sit here with me.'

He sat down and pulled her down beside him, right close into his arms.

'Close to me. I will have that comfort at least. My arms around you, darling Miranda.'

She lay, her head on his shoulder, quietly in his arms. She could smell the dampness of his clothes and the heat of his body and the fear that lay all round him. His heart thudded as he kissed her hair and the naked nape of her neck.

'Did he sit like this with you?' he whispered the words into her ear.

'Foolish Cathal,' she murmured.

'Did he call you my darling Miranda?'

She didn't answer, just buried herself more into his body.

'Go to sleep my darling Miranda and tomorrow morning will come and we will all be happy.'

'That only happens in fairy stories.'

'Don't argue . . . don't say a word. Just sleep. I want to feel you sleeping in my arms, that peace. I want to know peace.'

She did sleep, because she was young; because she still

121

believed in the inevitability of miracles; in the possibility of happiness.

He held her and stared at her and felt her breathing and the fire sank down and warm ashes were heaped in the grate and the air began to feel cold. The three figures were like statues and through the twitched corner of the curtains the darkness began to drain away from the sky.

'It's so many years since I sat up all night.'

Mr Martin's voice broke the silence.

'In fact I can't remember the last time. I must have been very young. It used to be such an exciting thing to do. See the dawn in.'

He got up very slowly from his chair and walked over to one of the windows. He pulled one curtain back, carefully tying it with its tasselled silk rope. The rain was over. It would be a clean and shining day. He pulled the next curtain with equal care. You could see the trees across the avenue silhouetted against the colourless sky.

'If that nice young man were still here he would play us a tune. Something lively. A bit of Gilbert and Sullivan maybe. I always enjoyed Gilbert and Sullivan. I sang in *The Pirates* once . . . oh . . . ah . . . long time, long . . . . He had a great way with that engine you know. Said his father had one the same. Nice chap.'

He moved around the room to the next window. The rings rattled along the brass rail as he pulled the curtain open.

'I liked him. The sort of straightforward chap it's pleasant to have around. Uncomplicated.'

He sighed.

His hands trembled as he knotted the rope. His face in the dim light was grey with fatigue.

'I knew a Harrington when I was up at Cambridge. Wonder if he was a relation. Must ask the lad the next time I see him.'

He walked to the third window, the big one giving out over the terrace and the lawn below.

The yellow silk curtains were faded along the edges with the years of summer sun. She had bought those silk curtains in

London, he suddenly remembered, the year after they were married; replaced Mother's brocade ones; green they had been, same colour as the palm tree.

She, Julia. Yes. Julia's yellow silk curtains.

For a moment his hands held their softness.

'He was an oarsman, if I remember correctly. Yes. Rowed for Jesus. I was an oarsman myself once. I think Harrington was in the Jesus boat the year we won the Bumps.'

He stood by the window frowning to himself, trying to hide the present in the veils of the past.

'Harrington.'

Fingers of blue light stretched out into the dark sky.

Below the terrace two men walked across the grass.

'Yes.'

He turned his back to the window, moved towards the two young people on the sofa.

His voice was brisk when he spoke.

'Tell you what we'll do tomorrow . . . today, I suppose I should really say . . . . Your father and I, Cathal, will take you to see the new plantation on Knocknashee. Spruce. Doing very well now. Lovely new trees, fresh looking, only so high . . . .' He measured with his hands. 'So high . . . but in five years . . . ten . . . . We planted a shelter belt of pine in a semi-circle round the new trees. You know how bad the wind can get up there. Yes. We'll do that if it doesn't come on to rain.'

He stood beside them both.

'I think that storm has cleared the air.'

He put his hand quite lightly on Cathal's shoulder.

'One day,' he said, 'we'll plant forests all down the slopes of the West. Imagine, just imagine the bare hills covered with trees, just as they used to be in the old days.'

He stood beside them both.

'A romantic notion.'

A voice spoke from the doorway.

Mr Martin turned, keeping his hand lightly still on Cathal's shoulder.

Cathal could feel the trembling of the hand. He didn't move, didn't look round.

'Quite practical I assure you.'

Mr Martin's voice was calm, in spite of his trembling hand. A man wearing a long brown coat stood in the door, behind him in the hall two shadows. He moved slowly into the room. They moved carefully behind him. They had guns in their hands. The man in the brown coat took in the scene; the two men and the girl still sleeping, the pale irrelevant lamps, the warm ashes in the fireplace.

'It's Major Martin we're looking for.'

He spoke the words very politely as if it were some social occasion.

'I'm afraid,' said Mr Martin, equally politely, 'he had to leave. He and his friend were called away.'

'What a pity. We've come a long way to see him.'

'It's strange time of day to come visiting.'

'These are strange times, Mr Martin. Even living out here in the back of beyond, you must be aware of that.'

'I am aware.'

'You keep late hours.'

Mr Martin nodded.

'Sometimes. Not often. I am getting on in years. I was in fact saying only a few minutes ago that it is a very long time since I saw the dawn in.'

'You will be pleased to get to your bed then. Just a few minutes and you can be on your way.'

'I'm not in any hurry,' said Mr Martin mildly.

'But we are. Before the world is up, we have business to do. Come along Dillon, don't let us keep the Martin family out of their beds any longer than is necessary.'

'Charlie is staying here. He is our guest, our good friend. Presumably you are aware of the name and meaning of this house?'

'I am indeed Mr Martin. In the past . . . .'

'He hasn't asked for sanctuary. I have offered it. Doesn't that mean anything any more?'

'Only to fools and innocents. The world is no longer as simple as you seem to think it is.'

'So my son tells me.'

'Your son knows what's what all right. There's no denying that.'

'I thought I might be able to tell you how good, how honourable, this young man is. I thought you might listen to me.'

'Informer. Traitor. Spy.'

'Oh dear me, no.'

'There are two sides to every coin, Mr Martin. I don't think you should interfere. There has been a serious breach of military discipline.'

'I know nothing about military discipline. Do you believe in God?'

'Hardly a relevant question.'

Cathal looked down and saw Miranda's open eyes staring up at his face. He smiled slightly and bent to kiss her.

'No,' she whispered.

'We just want to discuss a few things with you, Dillon. Are you ready to come?'

Cathal stood up.

'No.' She clutched at his hand.

'I can assure you,' said Mr Martin. 'Charlie has done nothing . . . nothing that cannot be discussed here in this room.'

'I'm ready,' said Cathal. 'Let's go. Let's go. Let's get this whole damn thing over with.'

'A sensible attitude, I must say. It's sensible not to ask for trouble.'

Miranda stood up.

'No. Please don't take him away. What can we do? What can we say. What can we give you?'

She moved towards the man in the brown coat, the red dress crumpled from her sleep.

One of the gunmen moved towards her.

'Go back please.' The man's voice was still pleasant, social.

'Back behind the sofa. We don't want anyone to get hurt. Contrary to what many people believe, Mr Martin, we don't like innocent people to get hurt. I believe you to be extraordinarily innocent.' He gestured with his head for Cathal to move towards the door.

Without a word Cathal crossed the room.

'Father! Don't let them take him.'

Her father waved his hands miserably in the air.

'He was right. Words have no meaning in this sort of situation. We are not your enemies.'

The man in the coat laughed.

'I am aware of your position, Mr Martin, but you must realise that breaches of discipline must be dealt with. Dillon has been quite foolish. I think that he would agree with me, wouldn't you?'

Cathal didn't speak.

'He swore an oath. We have to remind people that oaths cannot be broken. Commitment is until we have Freedom. Don't you think Freedom is a noble cause, Mr Martin? A cause to die for?'

He moved over to the table where Cathal had thrown the gun. He picked it up and put it into his pocket and dropped the bullets in after it.

'No point in leaving this behind.'

He smiled at Mr Martin.

'I'm sure a gentleman the like of yourself would have no use for it.'

'Anything,' said Miranda. 'Anything at all.'

Her father took her arm and held it close against his side.

'Your parents?' he asked across the room to Cathal.

Cathal nodded.

'Just tell them any kind of decent lie. You'll know what to say. I'm sorry.'

'Out,' said the man in the brown coat. 'Take him away.'

Cathal nodded almost casually towards Mr Martin and Miranda and turned and left the room. The men with the guns followed him. Miranda picked up his coat from the chair

126

where he had thrown it earlier.

'His coat.' She took a couple of steps towards the door.

'He won't need his coat.'

'He'll be cold. It's cold out. He'll . . . .'

'We'll take care of that. Just put it down and stay where you are.'

He walked over to the door and turned.

'Thank you Mr Martin. I don't like needless violence.'

He saluted and left the room. They listened to his steps cross the hall. They listened to the door open and close. Miranda ran to the window, there was nothing, no one to be seen, only trees against the sky and the sound of waking birds.

'Father,' she began to cry, to howl more like an animal. 'Father. No. No. No. Cathal. Oh God, God, God, God. Oh please God. No.'

The room was now almost light and she stood in the window, Cathal's wet coat clutched in her arms, the dim irrelevant lamps, warm ashes in the fire, shadows now starting to grow across the fields as the sun rose.

Doors were opening and closing, feet pattering, slapping, stumbling on the stairs; voices stumbling, whispering moved towards them, towards their silence. The girls, strange in their night clothes and their streaming hair, pushed their way through the door; stood gaping until Nanny moved her way through them to stand beside Miranda. She pulled the shawl from her own shoulders and threw it round the weeping girl. 'Something's been going on,' said the old woman. 'Give that coat here to me, child, you're all soaked holding it like that. Cars and men and people running in the darkness. The girls were frightened out of their wits. Give it to me, Miranda.' She tried to prise the coat from Miranda's hands, but her own fingers were not strong enough.

'I tried to warn you . . . .' She stared at Mr Martin. 'But you wouldn't listen. You're not wise with all your years. Look at the state she's in now.'

One of the girls in the doorway began to cry.

Nanny turned fiercely towards her.

'Away with ye back to your beds, if you can't make yourselves useful. Mary Kate, fill jars for the master's bed and Miss Miranda's. Stop that whimpering, Bridie, and take the lamps with you when you go, there's no point in wasting good oil on the daylight. You'll all catch your death of cold with the bare feet of you. Where's sense gone at all?'

She managed to pull the coat at last from Miranda's hand and let it fall to the floor.

'You're soaked through. Pull that shawl close around you. Come child, come here to the fire, come with Nanny, child. Dear heart, don't be crying like that.'

She coaxed Miranda over to the fireplace, to where her father was standing, like a statue, hardly noticing what was happening around him.

'I told you . . . . Time and time again I said leave that boy alone to make his way as best he can. There's no good ever comes of interfering with the way things are. I told you leave him alone. Didn't I tell you that?'

'Yes Nanny. You did.'

'Where's the point in giving people notions? Shush your crying my pet, my little darling. It will pass. God is good.'

'I hate God.'

Nanny took hold of her shoulders and began to shake her, gently at first, but then as hard as she could manage.

'Never say that.' She almost shouted the words as she shook.

'God is not good. God is terrible. Why? Why? Why?'

'Never, ever again, let you say a thing like that. He listens. He listens all the time. Never say it Miranda. Such wickedness.'

'Why? Why? Why?'

The old woman lifted her hand and hit Miranda across the face.

'Highsterics,' she said in Mr Martin's direction.

Miranda stopped crying, stood for a moment in silence and then put her hand up to touch her cheek.

'Never again say a thing like that,' said Nanny sternly.

'Even and I'm not here to chastise you for it.'

'Why Father?' She whispered the words.

Mr Martin shook his head.

'I have never found any answers,' he said.

He took her hands, pulled her close to him, kissed her hands, cold hands. Her face was bruised by tears.

'Is it our fault?'

He nodded.

'I suppose so.'

She began to cry again, quiet tears, rising and flowing.

His hands became wet with her tears.

'Could we have . . . could we . . .?'

'I don't think so my dear. I suppose we might have forced him to leave with the boys, but it wouldn't have helped him in any way. He knew that. Merely put off . . . merely given him time to think . . . . Given him pain. Pain.' He pressed her hands. 'Go with Nanny now, there's a good girl. Go to bed. Take her to bed Nanny.'

'I don't want to go to bed.'

'Yes, yes, yes, yes, yes.'

He waved his hands, dismissing her.

'Go to bed child.'

'Father . . . .'

'Come along Miranda. Do as you're told. A few hours' sleep . . . .'

'I won't sleep.'

'You never know what you'll do till you try.'

'I don't want to try. I want to stay awake forever. Father . . . .'

He had turned away from her.

'I must go and wake Dillon. I – he – we must go to the police.'

'The police,' said Nanny with contempt. 'A fat lot of use that little Jackie Sullivan will be. Come along now Miranda, leave your father in peace. Your bed'll be nice and warm and Nanny will sit beside you till you go off. You won't get him back you know, no matter how you go about it. Neither the police nor all the English army itself will get him back. Poor Mrs Dillon. You'd better hasten on below to poor Mrs Dillon and put your coat on against the wind. I don't want to have you falling ill on me as well as all the sorrow. Come.'

She led Miranda across the room. At the door she paused for a moment.

'When I have Miranda off I'll run down to Dillon's. Tell her that. She'll need someone there. Tell her Nanny'll be down.'

'I'll tell her Nanny.'

He bent slowly and picked up Cathal's coat from the floor and then his sodden hat from the chair on which he had thrown it when he came in the night before.

How can I tell them?

What can I say?

Indisciplined words jostled in his head.

I will knock on their door and when they open it surprised so early in the morning, I will offer them such grief.

God give me gentleness and them the strength to hear what I will be saying. Amen.

Miranda's bed was warm and soft. Nanny tucked her in and smoothed her hair, pressing her head deep into the pillows, then as she had promised she pulled up the wicker chair and sat by the bed and sang.

'"I mbeal Atha na Gár atá an stáid-bhean bhrea mhódhuil, 'Bfhuil a grua marna caorthainn agus scéimh ina cló geal . . . ."'

Miranda struggled against sleep; the betrayal of sleep; the inconstancy of sleep.

All I can do is keep faith, she thought.

'Ba Bhinne guth a béil-san ná'n cheirseach 's ná'n smólach.'

Forever.

That is all I can do.

That is the only possible thing that I can do.

She forced her eyes open and looked up at the ceiling, striped now with morning sun.

'God, help me to keep faith. Forever.'

130

She had to say the words aloud. She had to have them witnessed.

'Sssh,' whispered Nanny. 'Sleep pet, sleep.'

'Forever.'

''S ná'n londubh ar na'n coillte le soilse trathnóna.'

It was the song she knew I loved so much that she sang. The song about the fair maid whose mouth's soft music was sweeter than the thrushes or the blackbird's song. I can hear the echoes of it now in my head. I can hear the crumbling measures of her old voice quite close to me now.

If he had lived, what then?

Down all the years I have often asked myself that question. We might have outfaced the ghosts together; raised a spreading brood to fill this house. No idyll, mind you; idylls are for fairy tales.

On the other hand, that tentative love we had might have been dissipated by our separations. He might have moved towards politics, after the fight was over; shifted into that grey area where expediency nudges truth out of its way; where freedom becomes a slogan, rather than a possibility. I would have hated that. There was too much of my father in me for that to give me pleasure of any sort.

Such foolish speculation.

We have to live with reality.

I used to dream about his death; see in my mind the splintering bone, the blood. I heard no sound, just saw the yawning of his skull as the bullets broke into it.

Terrible dreams; but they softened with the years.

Sometimes now when I read the papers, hear the news on the wireless, I try to conjure up those dreams again, recreate the pain of the past.

I can't any longer.

My indifference to the events of the last few years, the re-stirring of the pot of violence, frightens me, even now as I

131

lie here. I suppose I must have destroyed in myself the power to feel passion, pity, rage.

My one hope is that God will forgive me for the wilful destruction of myself.

If He remembers.

Had Cathal's body ever been returned, or even been turned up years later by some Bord na Mona machinery, or pulled from the sea, I might have reassessed my promise to God. I might have opened my isolation to some other person. Maybe not; a promise is, after all, a promise and I'll have Nanny if not God to face in the next world.

I have known the embraces of no man.

I wait now with deep impatience for the deep embrace of death.

I have played my play for the last time.

I am so tired.

The day Thou gavest Lord . . .,

Have pity on us all.